"Sweeth___ ___ou would b___

Lucien's voice ___ ___laughter faded. "Marria___ ___ould be what?" The storm outside chose that minute to kick up, drowning out his reply. She sat up in the bed. "Did you say heaven? Lucien?"

He was silent for a long moment. "You remember how it was between us. What else would you call it?"

"Sex."

"No way, sweetheart. I've had sex, and that wasn't it."

Raine cautiously planted her big toe on the cold wooden floor. "Then what was it?"

"You move another muscle off that mattress and you'll find out...."

Wedded Blitz

Marriages made in moments!

Finding the perfect partner isn't easy….
Enter the Cupid Committee! Quietly, secretly,
but very successfully, this group of anonymous
romantics has set hundreds of unsuspecting
singles on the path to matrimony….

Take Tess, Emma and Raine. Three best friends
who made a pact: if they're still single when they
turn thirty, they have permission to play matchmaker
for each other! But they have no idea that Cupid is
about to deliver a lightning strike….

Three women, three unexpected romances in:

August 2001: *The Provocative Proposal* (#3663)
September 2002: *The Whirlwind Wedding* (#3716)
November 2002: *The Baby Bombshell* (#3723)

DAY LECLAIRE
The Baby Bombshell

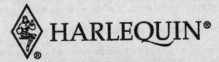
HARLEQUIN®

TORONTO • NEW YORK • LONDON
AMSTERDAM • PARIS • SYDNEY • HAMBURG
STOCKHOLM • ATHENS • TOKYO • MILAN • MADRID
PRAGUE • WARSAW • BUDAPEST • AUCKLAND

To Dr. Matthew Ellis and Erin O'Branski and all the
miracle workers at Duke University Medical Center,
with my love and thanks.

ISBN 0-373-03723-6

THE BABY BOMBSHELL

First North American Publication 2002.

Copyright © 2002 by Day Totton Smith.

This edition published by arrangement with Harlequin Books S.A.

Visit us at www.eHarlequin.com

Printed in U.S.A.

PROLOGUE

"I DON'T care what it takes, I want you to see to it that my granddaughter marries Lucien Kincaid."

Shadoe took a seat at the kitchen table. Shooting a quick look at his mother, he addressed the woman they'd flown in to meet. "Mrs. Featherstone—"

"Everyone calls me Nanna. I don't answer to anything else." She set a plate of oatmeal cookies and tall glasses of ice-cold milk on the table in front of Shadoe and Adelaide. While Adelaide had the intestinal fortitude to withstand Nanna's demanding stare, Shadoe suspected that if he didn't eat at least one cookie, there'd be hell to pay.

"Nanna," Shadoe tried again. "We appreciate that you'd like the Cupid Committee to spark a match between Raine and Lucien. But are you aware that your granddaughter isn't interested in getting married?"

"Of course she's interested." Nanna folded her arms across her chest. She was a tall, slender woman, with long graying hair looped around her head in a crown of braids. It was clear where her granddaughter, Raine, had inherited her good looks. At the very least, Nanna had passed on fine-boned features, clear green eyes and an iron will. "Anyone who claims different is either an idiot or a liar."

Shadoe cleared his throat. "Actually, Raine said it."

"I repeat. Anyone who claims different is an idiot or a liar, and that includes my granddaughter, much as I love her. No matter what she says, she's had a hankering for that Kincaid boy since she was old enough to know why bees buzz flowers.''

Adelaide chose that moment to step in. ''You understand that the Cupid Committee prefers to work in secret.''

'''Course I do. That's why everyone knows about you—because no one's supposed to.'' She joined them at the table and pointedly shoved the plate of cookies in Shadoe's direction. ''Raine told me how you matched Tess and Emma with their husbands. All I'm asking is that you do the same for Raine as you did for her best friends.''

''Regardless of her preferences?''

''She prefers Lucien. She's just too stubborn to recognize that fact. I guarantee that if you put the two of them together, nature will take care of the rest.''

''Lucien and Raine have known each other for a lot of years,'' Shadoe commented. ''The fact that they haven't acted on their feelings in all this time suggests that their interest is superficial.''

''Poppycock. They acted. Other matters got in the way before anything could come of it. They should have married a full decade ago. Would have, too, if Lucien hadn't made the mistake of killing my husband.''

Shadoe froze, a cookie halfway to his mouth. ''Excuse me?''

Nanna lifted an eyebrow. ''Didn't your research turn up that information?''

That single raised brow almost had him stammering out an abject apology. He caught himself just in time. ''I'm afraid we missed that detail.''

''Well, it's no secret, just a true tragedy. Paps Featherstone and Lucien got into a foolish tussle a dozen years back. Unfortunately, there was a shotgun in that tussle with them—Paps' fault, I'm sad to say—and there was only one man standing after all was said and done. It sort of chilled relations between our two families.'' Stark grief gleamed in her odd green eyes, belying her matter-of-fact tone. ''But the time's come to put the past behind us.''

Shadoe returned the cookie to his plate. ''Let me get this straight. You want Raine to marry the man responsible for the death of her grandfather?''

An ageless quality stirred in Nanna's gaze, a calm acceptance coupled with an immeasurable hope. ''Time can change a body's perspective on certain events.''

''I gather your perspective has changed.'' He hesitated. ''But has Raine's?''

Nanna's chin assumed a stubborn slant. ''Raine deserves happiness. She's spent the past eight years working nonstop in an effort to keep this place going. Her life's been one long sacrifice and it's time for that to end. There's only one way that's going to happen.''

''With a wedding.''

Nanna inclined her head. ''Lucien loves my granddaughter. He won't let her wear herself to a frazzle over something as unimportant as a piece of land. He'll also do whatever it takes to make her happy. And best of all, he'll give her babies. Lots of fat, happy babies that will bring laughter back to our two families. What could be better than that?''

Adelaide helped herself to a cookie. ''We've checked and I have to admit, it does sound like Lucien would make Raine a good husband, that one incident aside.''

''Then you'll set your cupids on 'em?''

''Within limits. We have a few conditions first.''

Nanna didn't hesitate. ''Fair enough. Name them.''

''First, our arrangement is to remain strictly confidential," Adelaide said. "The last time someone knew about the Cupid Committee's involvement in advance, it turned into a disaster."

"Amen," Shadoe muttered.

Adelaide smiled. "Fortunately, it did work out in the end. But it made our job next to impossible."

"I have no problem with that," Nanna said. "I'm no more interested than you in having Lucien and Raine find out what we're up to."

"Excellent. Second, we'll arrange matters so Lucien and Raine are thrown together. But the choice to act must remain theirs."

"Trust me. They'll act."

"And finally, if nothing comes of this one opportunity we create, we can't interfere further."

Nanna didn't look pleased. "You're only willing to give it one shot? Have you any idea how stubborn those two are?"

"One shot. Take it or leave it."

Nanna mulled it over as she helped herself to a cookie. "Put like that, I guess I'll take it."

Adelaide grinned, saluting Nanna with a glass of milk. "I thought you might. Now here's what we'll need...."

CHAPTER ONE

LUCIEN KINCAID eyed the angry sky and grimaced. Not the best day to be on horseback, miles from home. When he got his hands on Raine Featherstone, she was going to regret ever having sent him on this fool's errand. He encouraged his gray over the next rise with a soft click of his tongue and surveyed the Texas landscape. Lightning forked from sky to hillside, crashing to earth a few scant miles away. Following close on its heels came the rumble of thunder, booming eerily through the natural caves buried in the limestone substratum.

"What do you think, Poke?" he muttered. "That woman setting us up for a long drop off a short cliff?"

His favorite mount answered as horses were wont to do, with a shake of his bridle and a snort Lucien preferred to think of as disgusted agreement. But then, after years of close and frequent association, he figured he had a decent feel for his horse's opinions since they pretty much mirrored his own. Poke had always been wise in the ways of humans, treating them with a mixture of amused tolerance, coupled with a healthy dose of skepticism. But then, Poke was pretty damned smart.

In fact, the only thing the headstrong critter hadn't learned was that beautiful women weren't to be trusted. And beautiful women with hip-length black hair, pale green eyes and a bewitching voice were to be avoided at all costs. Not that Lucien could point many fingers. It was a lesson that had taken him quite a few years to master. Considering he'd come running the minute he'd received Raine's note, it would seem he hadn't mastered it all that well.

Poke snorted again and Lucien nodded. "Yup, that's what I think, too. She's up to something. The question is…" He yanked the brim of his Stetson low on his brow. "What?"

There was only one way to find out. Stripping off his gloves, he yanked a crumpled note from his shirt pocket. He knew what it said. Hell, he'd read it a dozen times or more. But he wanted one last gander to help set the tone for their meeting. As before, the bold, imperious words piled extra heat onto his already hot temper.

"Kincaid"—not Lucien like she used to say, blurring the syllables so they came out as a lazy caress—"meet me at the line shack. The one where you proved what a jerk you were back when we were kids." Jerk? His brows met across the bridge of his nose. That's how she referred to her one-time lover? And what the hell was this about being kids. They'd both been old enough to know better, just too horny to give a damn. "Five this afternoon. Be there or you'll regret it."

She'd signed the thing with a large, simple "R." No frills. No girlish swirls or cutesy curls. Just a single, peremptory letter. But then, that was Raine. He crushed the note in his fist before allowing the storm-driven wind to consume it. The scrap of white paper bounced along the scrub-covered ground as though driven by single-minded purpose. Knowing Raine, she'd imbued the thing with a fair dollop of her own ornery personality and it had no choice but to eat up ground in long, mean strides. He watched the wadded paper ball until it bolted out of sight down a rocky crevice, then returned his attention to the line shack.

It was buried beneath a huge slippery elm on the side

of a slope that tumbled recklessly toward a riverbed parched from a long, dry spell. A narrow ribbon of muddy water snaked in the general direction of the Balcones Escarpment, the flow building even as he watched. He lifted his gaze to the black clouds in the distance, clouds that were no doubt dumping a substantial downfall at the river's source. It wouldn't be long before the stream was in full flood.

"Come on. We've wasted enough time on this nonsense, old friend," Lucien informed his horse. He gave Poke a gentle nudge in the ribs. "Let's find out what she wants and get the hell home."

Beneath the widespread embrace of the elm, the shack appeared deserted and vaguely rundown. The wind kicked up as he approached, ripping at the branches and sending leaves and twigs skittering across the dented tin roof. If he'd had his druthers, he'd have neglected the thing right into the ground. But practicality had won out and he'd kept the cabin in reasonable repair for those few occasions when he or one of his employees needed a place to hole up for the night after too many hours riding fence or collecting stock. This part of his spread didn't take well to Jeeps or any other mode of transport other than his Poke. That made the shack a regrettable necessity.

Lucien rode right up to the front of the cabin and climbed off his horse, ground-hitching him. He and Poke had an agreement. Lucien didn't tie up Poke, and Poke stayed where he was put. Of course, the horse was fast approaching the age where he wasn't in any hurry to move, anyway, particularly when carrying an extra-large man on his back. If it weren't for an annoying streak of sentimentality—heaven only knew where that came from—Lucien would have retired the animal long ago.

Instead, he took the aging critter with him on short days when the work wouldn't prove too strenuous and they could enjoy a lazy chat along the way.

Thunder grumbled in the distance and Poke released a nervous whinny. Lucien glanced over his shoulder. "I know you don't like storms. But don't give me any grief, old friend. This is Raine's doing. You can give her a piece of your mind when she shows up." He adjusted his hat again. "Maybe I'll do the same."

Climbing the five warped steps to the door, he stumbled on the top one. Turning, he prodded it with the toe of his boot. A broad crack split the board in two and he made a mental note to get it fixed. Thrusting open the door to the shack, he checked inside. He knew what he'd find. No Raine. Sure enough, she hadn't arrived. He took a few steps into the cabin, the clip of his boot heels raising a hollow echo as they struck the dusty floorboards.

He hadn't been here in years, not since a hot summer night when he'd been young, foolish, and brimming with hormones, and the woman he'd been with had been younger, every bit as brimming, and pert near as much a fool as he'd been. He took a minute to look around. Other than needing a good cleaning, the place was in decent shape. The last line rider who'd visited had left it fully stocked. The ancient wood-burning stove appeared in good condition, and the cupboard shelves were lined with tins of a variety of products, most of which contained beans.

He walked further into the cabin, examining the floor and noting one corner where rain had leaked through. He'd make sure that was repaired before winter set in, as well as replacing the front step. He'd also check the condition of the small corral and storage shed before leaving. That way he wouldn't have dusted his saddle for nothing these past few hours. Through the nearest window he saw another bolt of lightning stab across the menacing sky.

This time when Poke whinnied in distress, a soft, feminine voice responded. "Easy, Poke-a-long." Magic cascaded through the liquid tones. "Nothing's going to hurt you."

Lucien felt the power of Raine's voice pour over and through him. He'd never understood his reaction to her, but it hadn't changed in all the years he'd known her. At the first quiet word, his body clenched in preparation, the muscles tightly corded as though in response to a threat or in answer to a primal urge. She unsettled him, even as she drew him, a siren who issued the sweetest of calls, one that he was powerless to resist, regardless of the personal danger.

Dammit! Why couldn't he hold her at a safe distance? When he received her note, he should have sent a reply telling her where to get off and then helped her along her way with the flat side of his boot. Instead, he'd turned as docile as a gelding and returned to the one place he'd sworn never to step foot again.

He crossed to the door of the cabin and leaned against the jamb. Raine stood close to Poke, her face buried in his, crooning softly in his ear. If it had been physically possible, his horse would have melted at her feet in a puddle of hooves, hide and horsey drool. Not that Lucien blamed poor Poke. Lesser beasts—hell, lesser men—had responded just that way.

Without question, she was a beauty. The women from whom she was descended always grew tall and proud, passing on to each subsequent generation the gift of thick black hair, a soul-shattering gaze, and an innate grace. But the attraction went deeper than that. Even as the decades passed and their eye color had transformed from coffee-brown to a more unsettling shade of pale green, one characteristic had remained constant.

From the moment they opened their mouths as babes, they enchanted everyone within hearing.

"You were supposed to give her a piece of your mind, you miserable hoss," Lucien grumbled beneath his breath. "Not kiss the skin off her."

Woman and beast turned as one to glare at him. "You left him out here all alone," she accused, flipping her braided rope of hair over her shoulder.

Lucien lifted an eyebrow. "What? You wanted me to bring him inside?"

"He's afraid of storms. He always has been." The magic she'd shared with his horse had disappeared from her voice, replaced by a backwash of emotions he'd become all too familiar with these past few years. "You should have stayed out here with him."

Poke snorted his agreement and Lucien fixed the turncoat with a grim look. "I suggest you reconsider your tone, old friend. Otherwise, you don't have a hope in hell of getting your usual bedtime treat."

The horse chewed on that one a spell, grinding the bit between his teeth. Apparently sugar lumps didn't rank as high on Poke's can't-survive-without items as Raine's gentle touch, because he buried his huge horsey face against her shoulder and blew out an ecstatic sigh. If she hadn't been a full five foot eight inches of lean strength, she'd have found herself knocked flat on the ground by the overwhelming display of affection. Raine's mare, Tickle, must have felt left out, because she closed in on Raine's other side, nudging for a bit of attention, as well.

It was the outside of too much. "Enough,

Featherstone.'' He jammed his Stetson low on his head, signaling his impatience. ''I want to get home before this storm breaks. Come inside and tell me what you want.''

As though his words had invited the inevitable, the first few drops of rain pelted from the sky, slapping her face. To his consternation, they slid down her cheeks like tears, stirring an inner turmoil. It didn't take much thought to understand where that turmoil originated. When it came to Raine, he still felt a lingering guilt mixed with an aggravating concern. He didn't care for either reaction, since he shouldn't give a damn about her anymore.

And yet, he did.

More raindrop tears slid down her face, making him realize he'd never actually seen her cry. Even at her grandfather's funeral, she'd maintained a stoic calm that certain less-than-kind souls had attributed to a lack of caring. He'd known better, known how desperately she'd loved her grandparents and how desperately she hated him for killing Paps. That's why he'd never told her the truth about the old man's passing. Even he wasn't that much of a low-down scoundrel. Fortunately, the only other two people who'd known the truth had long since died, ensuring the secret remained just that.

Raine rested a hand on each horse's neck. ''Feel free to speak your mind so we can get home, Kincaid. But we'll talk right here, if it's all the same to you.''

''It's not all the same to me. We'll talk inside.'' He didn't give her time to argue. Grasping her arm, he extricated her from between the two horses. She popped free like a cork from an overexcited bottle of champagne. ''Let's go.''

"Using brute strength isn't fair," she objected. "Especially when you possess so much of it."

"Tough." He ushered her up the stairs. "Watch where you plant your feet. Top board's loose."

"Such a gentleman. You must have made your grandmother proud."

The dig hit home, not that he allowed it to show. "We'll leave her out of this discussion, if you don't mind. I'd rather not speak ill of the dead during a lightning storm. Knowing her, she'd send a few stray bolts our way." Once they were inside the cabin, he faced her, folding his arms across his chest. "Now why did you drag me all the way out here? What the hell do you want?"

It was almost too dark to see her reaction, but what little he caught looked suspiciously like confusion. "What are you talking about?"

"I'm talking about the note you sent. The one asking me to meet you here."

She shook her head, the silky ends of her braid jangling about her hips. "You were the one sending notes, not me."

Intent on proving her a liar, he stripped off his gloves and shoved them beneath the belt at his waist. Thrusting his hand into his shirt pocket, he came up empty, remembering an instant too late that he'd tossed the message. "I threw your note away."

"Right."

"You don't believe me." No point in stating it as a question. The look of utter disbelief gleaming in her catlike eyes warned him of that. "You care to tell me what we're doing here, if you didn't send a message?"

"You sent the message."

Matching his movements, she stripped off her gloves,

shoving them beneath the belt at her waist. But when she slipped her hand into her shirt pocket, she came up with a neatly folded slip of white paper. It looked suspiciously familiar. A clap of thunder swallowed his graphic expletive.

As soon as the rumble had abated, she uncreased the note and read. "'Featherstone—get your ass up to the cabin. The one where we had a bit of fun a few years back.'"

She spared him a brief glance. For some reason, the green-gold color managed to express outrage better than any other shade of eyes he'd ever seen. Not that he blamed her. The note left him feeling a bit outraged, as well. Maybe more than a bit.

"I didn't write that," he stated.

"Funny. It sounds just like you. You have such a way with words, Kincaid. Some lucky woman must be thrilled right down to her neon-painted tippy-toes to have such a kind, respectful man in her life."

He addressed the most vile of the two slurs first. "I don't date women with neon-painted anything." He inclined his head toward the scrap of paper. "And I didn't write that note."

"No, of course not. Just like you didn't write, 'Be there by five or I'll make your life hell.'"

Lucien pushed words through his teeth. "I. Didn't. Write. That."

"Well, I don't know anyone else who calls me Featherstone in that tone of voice," she argued.

"Notes don't have tones of voices."

"This one does. I can hear it loud and clear. I also don't know anyone who'd use such a highhanded manner in ordering me up here. Or who'd be crude enough to refer to what happened all those years ago." Her gaze darted to the corner of the room holding the bed and back again. A hint of color touched her bronzed cheekbones, but she plowed on with determination. "Since you specialize in making my life hell and since the letter is signed with an 'L' as big and broad as every Kincaid male I've ever met, tell me who else could have written this note?"

He held out his hand, waiting until she reluctantly turned over the message. It was too gloomy to make out the words where he stood, so he crossed the room in order to take advantage of the waning light filtering in through the doorway. He studied the note for a long minute. The words read exactly as she'd claimed, the signature a large, striking slash across the bottom of the page.

Damn. If he didn't know better, he'd have sworn this was his handwriting. "Someone's setting us—"

A flash of light momentarily blinded him, the lightning bolt striking within yards of the cabin. It was followed by a deafening roar of thunder that jarred him straight through to the bone. It did more than that to Raine. It knocked her clean off her feet. Outside, Poke released a scream of terror and then bolted. If the sound of multiple fleeing hoof beats was any indication, Raine's mare followed close behind.

"Tickle, no!" she cried.

Regaining her feet, Raine shoved him aside, and rushed from the cabin. She landed full on the loose board at the top of the steps. It snapped in two, pitching her forward, and she teetered on the edge, pinwheeling helplessly for a split second. Lucien reacted out of sheer instinct. Diving forward, he caught her just as she toppled from her perch. Grabbing her around the waist, he twisted in midair so he took the brunt of the impact as they ate dirt. He landed with his left arm beneath him, his wrist and hand taking the full force of their combined weight.

He swore at the wrenching pain, the words quick and brutal. As though in response, the heavens opened, a wall of water flooding earthward in an icy deluge. Above him, Raine's slim body provided an interesting shelter from the elements while he cushioned her from the hard, rocky ground beneath—ground that was rapidly turning to a thick, sticky mud.

Raine didn't appear to appreciate being his shelter any more than she appreciated having him as a cushion. Elbowing him in the gut, she rolled clear. "Don't swear at me! You have no cause to do that."

"That wasn't aimed at you." Within seconds of their parting, they were both soaked through. Lucien checked his arm. Not a break, but definitely a bad sprain. Lightning ripped through the curtain of rain and he raised his voice, shouting to be heard. "Get inside. It's not safe to be in the middle of this. That last strike was close."

"You're hurt." She remained kneeling, the muddy ground beneath her fast turning into a quagmire. "Is it busted?"

"No." He levered himself upward. That was the trouble with being so damned large. There was more of him to hurt and this time he'd managed to bruise most of it. To his surprise she planted her shoulder beneath his arm and helped him regain his footing. "Thanks."

"Don't thank me. I wouldn't leave my worst enemy out in this." She glanced up at him, wry amusement penetrating her voice. "Come to think of it, you are my worst enemy."

"I always knew we were a perfect match. Just didn't realize what sort."

"Now you do. The bad sort."

Together they managed to climb the steps without incident. Crossing the threshold they stood just inside the open doorway. A puddle formed beneath them, the thick layer of dust from the floor swimming across the surface in muddy brown waves. Removing his Stetson, Lucien swept his damp hair back from his face before tossing his hat onto one of the pegs beside the door.

Raine followed suit, her hat twirling in a lazy circle beside his. "I gather we won't be leaving anytime soon?"

"Not without horses," he confirmed. "And not while that storm's taking out its wrath on half the county."

"Thought as much." She sent a final wistful glance over her shoulder. "Too bad I didn't bring Dog with me. I could have sent him after the horses."

Lucien snorted. "Oh, he'd have gone after them, all right. And then he'd have led the charge for home. Face it, Featherstone. We're stuck here, Dog or no Dog."

She wasn't any happier about accepting the inevitable than he was, but she swallowed it without more than a momentary grimace. It reminded him of the face she'd make when choking down one of her grandmother's flu tonics, which told him where he rated in the grand scheme of things.

"What now?" she asked.

He inclined his head toward the stove. "First we get the wood-burner going. Then we dry off."

"That should prove interesting." She examined it with undisguised curiosity. "How old is that thing, anyway?"

"Old enough to function without breaking down every five minutes and young enough to still work."

An actual smile tugged at her mouth. "Sounds like the perfect age."

He eyed his swollen wrist. "Sounds like an age I wouldn't mind experiencing for a change."

She frowned at his injury. "I think we'd better get your wrist taken care of before we tackle anything else." Looking around she located a shelf containing the bed linen. Helping herself to one of the pillowcases, she removed a small knife sheathed in her boot and sliced the cotton into strips. In a practiced move, the blade disappeared back into her boot. Returning to his side, she took his hand in hers. "Spread your fingers so I don't make it too tight," she instructed.

"You've done this before."

"Once or twice." Lightning flashed dramatically in the background as she wound the makeshift bandage around his hand, wrist, and forearm. "I wasn't very gracious earlier. Thanks for catching me."

"You're welcome."

"I'm serious." She paused in her labors, checking to make sure she hadn't cut off his circulation. "You saved me from a nasty fall. I'm just sorry you hurt your hand in the process. I feel bad about that."

"Don't let it bother you. It was my choice to play the part of the hero. I'm just not very good at it."

"Lack of practice, no doubt." She bit the ragged end of the bandage and ripped it in half. Looping the two ends around his wrist, she knotted them. "You hurt anywhere else?"

It wasn't a question he cared to answer. Truth be told, he hurt all over. But the biggest ache of all came from standing too close to Raine. It forced him to inhale her scent. To hear her singular voice. To stand calm and impassive beneath her gentle touch when what he really wanted was to shove her across the room and onto the bed they'd once shared and become reacquainted with every glorious inch of her. Maybe it was the storm putting such elemental thoughts in his head. The lightning electrified the atmosphere, while the thunder growled out a hungry demand. Whatever caused the problem, resistance was becoming increasingly difficult.

When he didn't respond to her question, she lifted an inquiring gaze to his. "Hurt?" she prompted. "Yes or no?"

He shrugged. "I'll live." Sorer but wiser, same as always.

"We still haven't discussed how we came to be here."

"That'll have to wait. You're starting to turn blue around the edges. I want to get that stove up and running before anything else."

"Fine."

One of the things he'd always admired about Raine was that she didn't expect to be coddled or waited on. She pitched right in and accomplished whatever needed doing. Braving the thunder and lightning, she stepped onto the porch and grabbed a split log from the pile leaning against the outer wall and tossed it to him through the open doorway. He caught each one with his good arm and dumped it beside the stove. Within minutes they had enough wood to get them through the night.

By the time he'd fired up the stove, Raine had filled and lit the two kerosene lanterns she'd found beneath the sink and placed them at opposite ends of the cabin. She'd also stuck a bucket under the damaged section of roof and used a spare length of manila to string a clothesline from wall to wall. On the shelves closest to the bed, she collected a blanket and a set of sheets. She draped the blanket over the line.

"Your side," she said, pointing to the section closest to the door. She tossed him one of the sheets, tucking the other beneath her arm. "You stay put and we might get through this."

He eyed her from his crouched position by the stove. "We're gettin' through this whether I stay put or not."

She instantly locked horns. But then, he'd pretty much figured she would. "There's getting through, and then there's getting through," she warned. "Keeping that rope between us means waking up tomorrow hale and hearty. Fool with that blanket and you'll wake up in a world of hurt."

He grinned. "Might be worth it."

"Trust me, it won't."

She disappeared behind the blanket and he heard one of her boots hit the floor. The other one must have caused her a bit of trouble. He could hear her hop up and down on one stockinged foot as she tugged at the stubborn boot, her breath escaping in annoyed grunts. After a minute the boot appeared beneath the bottom edge of the blanket.

"Would you mind?" she asked.

"Not at all." He cupped the heel with his uninjured hand and gave the boot a good hard tug. It slipped free and he passed it back to her.

"Thanks."

The magic had returned to her voice and he responded to it with impressive speed. Every muscle in his body quickened, tension humming just beneath the surface. Her voice called for him to act, and he wanted to. Badly.

But the only possible action would put him on the wrong side of that blanket and into the world of hurt she had waiting for him.

The clunk of her belt buckle hitting the wooden floor dispelled the momentary enchantment.

He knew he should be shedding his own wet clothes, but somehow he couldn't work up the energy to do it. He was too fascinated by what was happening behind the thin layer of wool separating them. Next he heard the metallic rasp of her zipper. A moment later she flung her jeans over the line closest to the wood-burning stove. Water trickled from the heavy denim, the staccato drip a fitting accompaniment to the noisy downpour pounding against the tin roof.

Lucien wished he could see her legs, see if they were as toned and shapely as he remembered. Did she still wear plain white cotton underwear? Or had she switched to silk? Maybe red silk. An image of feminine bits of flaming red draped against her elegantly bronzed skin tones exploded in his brain, and he lowered his head, shaking it. But the fantasy he'd summoned wouldn't be dispelled no matter how hard he tried. Instead the details grew clearer and he had a perfect picture of tiny scraps of material clinging to her high, rounded breasts and cupping the shadowed delta between her thighs. His body seized at the image and he swore beneath his breath.

"You cussing again, Kincaid?"

Aw, hell. "Might have been."

"Is your wrist bothering you?" She draped her cotton shirt next to her jeans. Heaven help him, that meant she was down to those frilly bits and pieces from his fantasy. "There's a bucket under that leaky section of roof. Once it's collected some rainwater, you can soak your wrist in it. It won't be as cold as ice, but maybe it'll help.''

"Yeah." The word escaped as more of a groan. And maybe he'd choose a more drastic solution and stand outside in all that cold rainwater until he'd regained his self-control. Shouldn't take long. Only a century or two. "I'll get right on it."

"Are you being sarcastic?"

"Not me."

"I was just trying to help." She poked her head around the edge of the blanket. "You're still dressed."

His brain finally kicked into gear and he managed to come up with a reasonable excuse. He lifted his bum hand. "I can't get my boots off with this wrist acting up."

"You should have said something before." She came around the blanket, the spare sheet wrapped around her like a sarong, not a hint of red silk showing anywhere. "Sit down and I'll pull them off."

Would she also help with his jeans? He knew better than to ask. If he were that much a fool he'd no doubt find himself sprawled spread-eagle in the mud on the wrong side of the cabin door, wondering what the hell had hit him. She continued to look at him, one eyebrow lifted in inquiry and he obediently took a seat on one of the cabin's two ladder-back chairs.

Raine knelt at his feet and grasped his boot with a fine-boned hand. With a quick yank she had first one, then the other pulled free. Gathering them up, as well as her own, she carried the mud-caked boots to the door and lined them up along the wall. His size sixteens dwarfed her puny eights.

She stared down at them with an amused expression on her face. "I never realized what big feet you have."

"When I kept growing, so did they."

"Makes sense." She turned to confront him. "You need to get out of your clothes. I assume you can take care of it even with that wrist?"

"And if I can't?"

"Make do. You've been busted up worse than this and managed."

"You gonna stay and watch?"

"Not a chance."

She returned to her side of the blanket. In typical fashion, she didn't hurry or act flustered. All her movements were calm and easy. Matter-of-fact. It annoyed the hell out of him that he felt as randy as a schoolboy while she didn't seem to notice he existed. If he were a man of less control, that blanket would be heaped in the dust with her neatly sandwiched between it and six foot four inches of rampaging male. In fact, the more he thought about it, the more the idea appealed.

With a frustrated groan, he stood and yanked at the row of snaps holding his shirt closed. They popped open from throat to belt buckle. Gingerly, he stripped off his plain blue work shirt and crossed to the makeshift clothesline to add it to the growing row of wet clothing. Standing this close he had a perfect view over the top. Raine sat cross-legged on the bare mattress. She'd loosened her saturated braid and a waterfall of ruler-straight hair tumbled across her shoulder to pool in her lap. Her fingers were caught within the turbulent flow, combing through the ink-black strands.

He swallowed, shoving out the handful of gruff words that were all his beleaguered brain could manage. "Come sit closer to the stove or you'll never get that mane of yours dry."

He'd caught her by surprise. She glanced up and

froze, as though something about the innocuous demand had alerted her to his state of arousal. Her pale eyes were filled with the sort of womanly vulnerability that normally stayed well hidden from the likes of mortal man. But he saw it plain this time and it only made him want her all the more.

Right then and there, he made a vow, one he'd move heaven and earth to keep. No matter what it took, this night would end with her in his arms.

CHAPTER TWO

DON'T just sit there, Raine ordered herself. Move. Say
something innocuous. Do something to ease the tension.
Just stop staring at his shoulders! Thunder boomed a
warning and she jumped, knocked from her trance.

"You're not supposed to come onto my side," she
informed him. Brilliant, Featherstone. Considering he
wasn't on her side, she'd just given him the perfect
opening to indulge his peculiar brand of humor.

Lucien recognized it, as well. Eyes as black as a
moonless night gleamed with a hint of laughter and a
half smile tugged at the corner of his broad mouth. She
recognized that look. It was an irresistible mixture of
devilish charm and "gee, shucks, ma'am" good ol' boy
appeal. Danger and good-natured fun. That deadly combination had succeeded in coaxing at least half the
women in the county into his bed.

"Want to try again?" he offered. "Maybe hit me with
a comment along the lines of, 'Don't look at me like
that, you dirty rotten scoundrel'?"

"Sounds good to me, considering that's precisely
what you are." She returned to sliding her fingers
through her hair, concentrating on making the motion as
smooth and relaxed as possible. "You're not supposed
to invade my side."

"In case you hadn't noticed, I'm still on my side of
the rope."

Technically, he was right. Still... Naked shoulders rip-
pling with lean muscle qualified as an invasion in her

28

book, especially when they'd leaked over the top of the blanket and were busy infiltrating her every thought and desire. "Crossing the line includes using your height to unfair advantage."

"I'm just worried about you getting warm and dry."

"That's none of your concern. You just worry about staying put."

His smile faded, along with every scrap of charm and fun. Only the danger remained. "I don't give a damn whose side is whose. Right now I'm more concerned about you turning into a human Popsicle." He jerked his head in the general direction of the stove. "Now haul your backside over here and quit acting like some outraged virgin from the turn of the century."

He knew how to hit where it hurt. Unfolding herself from the mattress she stalked toward the wool barrier separating them. "Since you relieved me of my virginity all those years back, I can't very well play the part, can I? But at least allow me a bit of outrage. You owe me that much."

"Outrage?" A rumbling quality crept into his deep tones, like the warning growl of a mountain lion. "Over what? You wanted me in your bed and I was only too happy to accommodate you."

Pain ripped through her. "Right. Out of the goodness of your heart." She wouldn't show how deeply he'd wounded her. Pride came to her rescue and she lifted her chin to a combative angle. "You're so kind, Kincaid. A regular prince among men. Too bad you were such a loose-lipped prince."

Lucien knocked the blanket aside. "Explain that crack."

The growl had turned to a full-throated roar and Raine couldn't help falling back a step. Even in a temper he was magnificent. He'd always been magnificent. It wasn't his size alone, although she found that impressive enough. It was also the formidable power of his personality and his sheer untamed maleness. She'd never encountered another man to match. The closest she'd come was during an accidental confrontation with a wild stallion.

The horse had broken free from its handlers and charged into the corral where she'd been working with a skittish mount. She'd turned at the thunder of hoof beats, placing herself protectively between stallion and mare. For the first time in her life she'd been uncertain of how to handle an animal. The stallion had been infuriated, determined to attack anything and everything in his path. The look in his reddened eyes spoke of an indomitable spirit and a refusal to bend to anyone's will. But what she remembered most was the scent that had filled the air, a scent that was sheer male virility.

Her mare had responded to that scent, as well, screaming in either fear or attraction. Raine couldn't tell which, though gazing at Lucien in all his male glory, she suspected it was a combination of both. A scent similar to the one she'd detected all those years ago teased her senses and she reacted the same way she had then.

She murmured something in a low voice, words designed to soothe and calm. She had no idea what she actually said. It wasn't important. Only the tone mattered. Lucien reacted just as the stallion had, falling back and shaking his head in momentary confusion. The heavy muscles spanning his shoulders and upper arms spasmed, the instinct to respond to her voice fighting an equally strong instinct driving him toward action.

He remained with his head bowed, his hands folding into fists. "Stop it, Raine," he ordered thickly.

"It'll be okay, Lucien."

He shook his head again. Raindrops scattered from his damp hair. They landed on the stove, hissing softly like a serpent's warning. His willpower proved phenomenal. He gathered himself up and looked at her, his eyes burning with a heat that shocked her. "I'm not one of your creatures. Don't handle me."

He was right and she strove to speak normally, finding it almost as difficult an accomplishment as he found resisting her words. "I can't always help it. It's a reflex."

"A reflex…when?"

She made a production of adjusting her sheet, not that it got her off the hook. He held his ground, clearly waiting for her response. Finally, she shrugged. "It just happens."

"When?"

"Whenever I feel threatened."

He didn't like her answer. With notable deliberation, he fell back a step. "You think I'd hurt you?"

"Physically?" She shook her head. "No. But you've hurt me in other ways. That's not a lesson I'm likely to forget."

He didn't pretend to misunderstand. "You mean the Disputed Land. Get over it, Raine. It's Kincaid land now."

"It belongs to the Featherstones," she shot back. "My grandfather spent his life fighting to get that land back after crooked politicians snatched it away the first time. It took his death for him to succeed. I'm not about to let you steal it again without a fight."

Pain swept across his face before all emotion vanished. "I'm not going to argue with you, Raine. Nanna agreed with me over the ownership of the Disputed Land. That ends the dispute."

"Sure she did. Right after you had that private conversation and applied who knows what sort of pressure. Just out of curiosity, what did you threaten her with? A nasty court fight? A battery of high-powered lawyers? You know she couldn't afford to fight you."

His mouth tightened. "I don't know why I'm bothering, but…I didn't apply any pressure. If you doubt me, ask Nanna."

She had asked and her grandmother had simply said that the land belonged to Lucien and she wouldn't discuss it further. Raine didn't know which topic of conversation she found more distressing—a discussion about their personal relationship, or about Paps and the land. Both cut deep, and in an odd way were intertwined.

When Lucien had loved her and then walked away, he'd taken from her something irreplaceable, something that went beyond the mere physical and struck right at the heart and soul of her nature. He'd tarnished what had once been beautiful and precious. By taking her land, he'd stolen a piece of her heritage. But when he'd accidentally shot Paps in a pointless argument over property lines, he'd killed her spirit. She'd lost both the men she'd loved that day and it still ate at her soul.

Raine confronted Lucien, driven to fight back even when the cause was hopeless. Something in her nature wouldn't allow her to back down. She'd never been one to bend when she could lay hands on a weapon—even if those weapons were no more than a quick wit and cutting words. "You took advantage of an old woman. Your grandfather gave Nanna that land after Paps died. She even has a letter to prove it. And when I find that letter, I'm dragging you into court and taking back what rightly belongs to the Featherstones."

"There is no letter to find."

"Everyone knew Buck Kincaid gave that land to Nanna. It was your grandmother who claimed it was a lie." Raine folded her arms across her chest, hugging the sheet to her. An uncomfortable coldness settled over her, partially from their conversation, but also from the dampness of her undergarments. "Of course, she conveniently waited until after your grandfather had died so he wasn't in a position to call her a liar to her face."

With an exclamation of impatience, Lucien strode toward her. Ducking under the clothesline, he wrapped an arm around her and propelled her toward the woodburning stove. Grabbing the nearest chair, he dropped it in front of the stove.

"Sit."

"Stop ordering me around, Kincaid." She fought free of his hold, well aware that the only reason she succeeded was because he chose to release her. "I'm not your property."

"You're going to stubborn yourself right into a sickbed. And if you do that, who's going to look after your place? Nanna?"

Darn him! The fact that he'd hit on the one argument guaranteed to win her cooperation frustrated her no end. Practicality won out. Turning the chair to a right angle to the stove, Raine took a seat. Flipping her wet hair over the shoulder closest to the heat, she resumed the process of combing the strands into some semblance of order. The task proved calming and the minute she'd regained her self-control, she flicked a glance in his direction.

"What about you? Those jeans are soaked through. Aren't you going to take them off?"

"You want me to strip? I'm happy to oblige."

His hands dropped to his belt and with swift, economical movements he released the buckle and shucked everything right down to his skin. She shouldn't stare. But there wasn't a chance in hell she had sufficient willpower to look away. Lamplight flickered across the tightly corded tendons of his nude body and something elemental quivered to life in the pit of her stomach, a blossoming need undimmed by time and circumstance. It swept through her, raging with all the wild ferocity of the storm overhead. She shook her head in bewilderment. How was that possible? How, when year after lonely year had turned their passion to bitter ashes, could desire rekindle with such wondrous heat and energy? After all he'd done to her, how could she still want him?

Perhaps it was a simple physical response. Biology or chemistry or something equally foolish. She attempted to consider it dispassionately. After all, his body had changed over the years. Maybe that explained her reaction. He'd always been built on a large scale, taller and broader and more muscled than most men she knew. But time had added other, highly appealing, dimensions.

He'd grown into his size, all the various parts coming together in stunning symmetry. His feet were large, true, but they carried a man whose legs were long and powerful, his thighs and flanks built for stamina and endurance. Though his hips and waist were comparatively narrow, his chest matched his legs, the impressive expanse as broad as it was deep. He'd also grown leaner over time, honed by grueling work into an instrument of perfect strength. He was a man capable of moving mountains in the literal sense, as well as through sheer dint of his personality.

He turned slightly and she caught a glimpse of a vicious scar streaking across his side. The sight caused her throat to tighten and she gestured toward it, struggling to sound offhand. "When did you pick up that little nick?"

He snapped open the sheet. "Sometimes the man wins and sometimes it's the bull."

His reply was surprisingly terse and she frowned. "I've seen the hurting end of a goring. That doesn't look like one."

He spared her a questioning glance. "You sure are giving a lot of attention to something you claim doesn't interest you. Keep staring and I'm gonna think you like what you see."

She shrugged. "I do like it, despite the scars." What normal woman wouldn't? "I'm just not interested anymore."

He settled the sheet at his hips, tying it with brisk efficiency. "Your head's not interested," he contradicted. Picking up his wet clothing, he tossed the various pieces onto the line. "The rest of you has a somewhat different opinion."

How did he do it? It was as though he saw straight through to her thoughts and emotions, reading them with distressing ease. "What makes you say that?" she whispered.

He approached and she fought to hide her reaction, continuing to comb her hair while keeping her posture as relaxed and natural as possible. Pausing by her chair, he touched a single finger to a spot just beneath her ear. Then he traced downward along the side of her neck.

"Your heart is pounding."

She swallowed. Light and easy, now. She just had to keep the conversation light and easy. "It has a tendency to do that," she explained. "I don't even have to lift a finger. It pounds away all on its lonesome."

"Cute." His finger drifted along the curve of her

shoulder, dropping to trace the edge of the sheet. "And your muscles are tensed as if you're tempted to run."

She was tempted. If she were asked, she'd have to say the storm raging outside seemed far safer than the one she faced by remaining here. "There's a reason for that."

"Which is?"

Levity faded, replaced by bone-deep honesty. "You're a threat."

His mouth curved upward in amused acknowledgment. "No more than you are."

She eased from beneath his touch. "Then I suggest we keep our distance from each other and maybe the threat will go away."

"One problem with that."

"Which is?"

"There's only one stove."

It took an instant for his answer to sink in. The minute it did, her lips twitched. She couldn't help it. Her breath escaped in a soft laugh as her sense of the ridiculous took hold. "Fair enough, Kincaid. Hunker in as close as you dare and we'll see if we can't manage to keep our hands off each other. Think it's possible to do that and conduct a civil conversation at the same time?"

"Keep my hands off you? No. Conduct a civil conversation?" He hooked his foot around the extra chair and angled it close to the stove. "I suppose that depends on how long the storm lasts."

She deliberately ignored his response to the hands-off part of her question, focusing instead on the second aspect. "We just have to be choosy about our topics of conversation."

"I suppose discussing our workday is out."

Her voice hardened. "Count on it."

He tilted the chair onto its back legs. "Normally the weather would be a safe topic."

As though his words had provoked it, the downpour drumming against the tin roof increased in ferocity. The branches from the slippery elm overhead pounded for entrance, leaves and twigs skittering around, no doubt looking for a convenient opening. She shot an uneasy glance toward the rafters. Just how well built was this shack, anyway?

Lucien intercepted the direction of her gaze. "It'll hold," he reassured. "These things are built to withstand nature's worst."

"Even so, discussing the weather doesn't strike me as the least safe," she replied, "considering it was the storm combined with your note that has us trapped here."

"Good. The note. We'll talk about that."

"That shouldn't take long."

"I think it's gonna take longer than you suspect."

"Only if you argue with fact." Finally. A topic that would take her mind off both the storm as well as the mountain of manhood sprawled so tantalizing close. "Admit it. It's all your fault we're stuck here. If you hadn't sent that note, we wouldn't be in our current predicament."

The front two legs of his chair hit the floor with a bang. "I'll say this one last time. I didn't send you anything. Not a note. Not a letter. Not so much as a single solitary word."

"I know your handwriting, Lucien. I should. I was on the receiving end of enough of your notes when you took over our land." She didn't bother mentioning the other times she'd received messages from him. Those had come during a brief lapse in judgment that she preferred to blame on her impetuous youth. Of course, those communications had been of a far different sort, the pages overflowing with tender words. Hot words. Words that left her pacing her bedroom in long, hungry strides, trying to outwalk an itch that only one man could satisfy. "I'd recognize that chicken scratch of yours anywhere."

He leaned forward in his chair, resting his forearms on his knees. His right wrist appeared painful beneath the bandage, not that he paid it any nevermind. Right now, she'd bet half her ranch the injury didn't exist for him. That ability amazed her. Although she tried not to dwell on life's more grievous lessons, she didn't have his capacity for ignoring pain.

Still, Raine had to give him credit. Lucien always had a knack for boxing up matters that didn't please him. Once sealed away, the problem no longer existed. What sort of box had he put their relationship in? she couldn't help but wonder. The large sort that kept getting in the way and you were constantly stubbing a toe on? Or a small, shabby cardboard affair, that could be tossed to the back of the closet and easily forgotten? She knew which hers was in. Her big toe throbbed just thinking about it.

"I saw that note you received and I agree with you," he surprised her by admitting. "It did look like my handwriting. Just like the handwriting on the message I had looked like yours."

She studied him in silence for a long moment. He met her gaze with unflinching calm. He was serious. She hadn't given much thought to his explanation earlier. There hadn't been sufficient time with so much happening so fast. But now that she listened to him and could weigh his claim, she realized that little about their situation made sense.

"What did my note to you say?" she asked.

"Enough to get me here."

Interesting. Either it said something to tick him off or the note had piqued his interest. Considering the underlying anger she'd sensed when she first arrived, she'd have to go with her first guess. Too bad. Lucien in a temper wasn't something she cared to confront again. Fortunately, his annoyance had eased, though she suspected it wouldn't take much to set a match to it again. He didn't suffer opposition well.

"I assume it was along the vein as what I received," she guessed.

"You assume right." He continued to watch her, his eyes narrowed in consideration. "Let's think about this. Who would you guess wants to trap the two of us here, together? And how would they benefit from it? It would have to be somebody willing to go to extremes."

An idea occurred, one so outrageous that she couldn't conceal her reaction. The Cupid Committee! Was it possible? Had they decided to play the sort of games with her that they'd played with Tess and Emma?

"What?" Lucien demanded. "You've thought of something. What is it?"

She couldn't tell him. No way, no how. What was she supposed to say? She could just imagine his reaction if she claimed, "There's this insane group of matchmakers all intent on working behind the scenes to arrange marriages between people. And guess what? We're next on their list."

It sounded preposterous. Besides, why would the Cupid Committee think she and Lucien had anything in common? They were closer to enemies than friends, and had been for years. Their type of relationship didn't bode well for a serious connection, particularly of a romantic nature.

"Spill it, Raine. What's going on?" he asked.

His voice had dropped a notch and she took the hint, offering the only response she could—a flat-out lie. "It's nothing."

He called her on it without hesitation. "Bull," he stated flatly. "You know, and one way or another you'll give me the answer I want. Don't push me on this, sweetheart. You won't like the results."

No, she wouldn't. She'd seen Lucien at his most ruthless when he'd claimed ownership of Featherstone land, and it had left a lasting impression. Getting between him and what he wanted wasn't a safe place to be. The emotional bruises inflicted when she'd found herself in just such a position still hadn't faded from their last go-round. "You don't understand. It's a thought I had, but it's impossible. Ridiculous, even."

"Who did this?" A dangerous quality threaded through the gravely tones, warning that his temper was wearing thin. "Answer me, Raine."

Great. She'd managed to rile him. A storm raged outside, another in, and she'd somehow gotten trapped between the two. "I think someone's playing a prank on us."

"Who?"

"The Cupid Committee."

He stared blankly. "Come again?"

She hitched the sheet higher on her breasts. "It's this crazy group based in Seattle. Tess and Emma know some of them."

"Your college friends?"

She nodded. "Yes. I was at their weddings recently and I think they might be involved."

"Let me get this straight. Your friends—your best friends—somehow arranged to send notes to the two of us in each other's handwriting. And they planned it for right before a storm hit so we'd end up trapped here. Is that the cock-and-bull story you've come up with?"

She flipped her hair back over her shoulder. "Tess and Emma didn't do it. Not by themselves. I think this Cupid Committee might have arranged it. If you knew some of the other stunts they've pulled with Tess and Emma, you'd understand."

"And this committee's goal is...?" He lifted an eyebrow.

Raine shook her head. No way was she answering that one. Let him figure it out playing with his own marbles. "Beats me."

"What did they do to Tess and Emma?"

She shot to her feet and paced toward the door, opening it a crack. "Do you think the storm is lessening? I'll bet if we poked around we could find some flashlights. It wouldn't take long to walk home."

"Only most of the night." The creak of his chair warned that he'd stood, as well. "And while we didn't have any trouble crossing the river on our way up here, it won't be as easy getting back."

"Then I suggest we get started."

"Not a chance." His voice tracked closer and she turned to confront him. His back was to the stove and she couldn't make out his expression. "The minute Poke returns without me, my men will send out a search party."

The door came alive in her hands, fighting like a bucking bronc. She fought back, struggling to latch it. "They'll come out in this?" she asked in surprise.

"No." She could see his face now and what she read

there did little to reassure her. He was a man after answers, answers he intended to get. ''You know better than that.''

He reached past her, his bare arm brushing her shoulder in a forbidden caress. Sensations rocketed through her, not that he seemed to notice. He slammed the door against the gusts of rain-laden wind, sheer muscle prevailing where her less powerful efforts had failed. The storm took out its anger on his impudence, sending half the scrub brush in Texas to attack the tightly shut door. Their needle-sharp branches clawed for entrance, making an unsettling counterpoint to the hot desire clawing at her for escape.

''Your men will wait until the storm passes and then come for us?'' she asked hopefully. ''Tonight?''

''Wrong again.'' He continued to stand next to her, torturing her with his closeness. ''They'll wait until morning.''

The instant his response sank in, she fought a wave of panic. His men would show up on their doorstop at daybreak. That meant… ''They'll trail us here?'' Why hadn't she thought of that? She'd realized from the first that she'd be stuck with Lucien for the night, but it had never occurred to her that anyone other than the two of them would learn of it. ''They'll find us together?''

He shrugged. Shifting from his stance, he distanced himself just enough to allow her to breathe again. ''Unless one of us has done the other in before they show up, then, yes. They'll find us here. Together.''

She could just imagine what they'd say when they discovered the two of them had spent the night in a one-room shack with a bed built for two. Of course, the bed was only built for two if those doing the sharing planned to sleep locked in a close and intimate embrace. Her gaze slid to the far side of the cabin and flinched from the sight of the bare mattress. Whether they actually used it or not, there'd be speculation. And laughter. Not to mention off-color comments. She set her jaw. Well, she'd heard it all before and it hadn't killed her. It might give her pride a dent or two, but nothing she couldn't handle.

"Take it easy, honey." Lucien must have picked up on the direction of her thoughts. A grim understanding darkened his eyes to jet. "The first man who says anything untoward won't be chewing for a long time to come."

Shock held her perfectly still. "What do you mean?"

"You know what I mean. The first man who says anything about tonight—whether it's in my hearing or out—will be looking for his teeth somewhere other than in his mouth."

"Why?" The muscles in her jaw were knotted so tight the words had trouble escaping. "You never cared about my reputation before."

Somehow she'd insulted him. She couldn't quite figure out how, but she saw it in his eyes and expression and stance. "Sure I cared," he informed her. "You think this busted nose of mine was from a bar brawl?"

"Yes."

He shrugged. "Well, yeah. I guess it was. But since you were the subject of the conversation at the time, I tend to credit you with the results."

She remembered hearing about that particular brawl. It had been vicious enough that Lucien had spent the night cooling his heels in the local pokey under Sheriff Tilson's auspices. "Your fight with Buster was about me?"

"It doesn't matter anymore."

"It does to me."

"You've managed to change the subject." He shook his head. "I don't know how you do it, but it's got to have something to do with that damned voice of yours. I start listening to it and every other rational thought goes clean out of my head."

"Not for long," she muttered. He differed from most in that.

"No. Not for long." He continued to hold his ground, not moving any closer, but not backing off, either. "You were about to tell me the purpose of this so-called Cupid Committee. What did they do to your friends, Raine?"

"Can't you guess?" She yanked at the tails of her sheet again. With her luck she'd step on one of the trailing ends and walk right out of the blasted thing. The minute Lucien stopped laughing his fool head off, he'd be on her like pillow ticking over goose down. "The Cupid Committee arranges matches."

"Matches, as in dates?"

"Sort of."

He made the connection an instant later. "Hell's bells, Raine. Are we talking matches as in marriage?" He stared at her in disbelief. "Someone's trying to matchmake us? Us?"

CHAPTER THREE

RAINE frowned. Did Lucien have to look so appalled? "I guess a few of the committee's matches end in marriage," she admitted.

Or maybe all of them. Hadn't Tess mentioned something about a perfect record? Only, it was worse than that. Raine struggled to recall details she'd given scant attention to at the time. If she remembered correctly, every romance this committee had ever orchestrated had ended in marriage, which added up to some astonishing number in the low three hundreds. Well, if they really were the ones behind the events that had set her on a collision course with Lucien, they were about to experience their first failure.

"Why would this group think the two of us would make a suitable couple?" he asked.

"I haven't a clue. If they'd bothered to ask me— which they didn't—I could have explained as much."

He continued to study her for an endless moment. "You're serious, aren't you? There really is this committee and they really do match people."

"Let's just say that Tess and Emma don't have any doubts about the committee's existence."

An odd expression flickered across his face. "This matchmaking outfit found them husbands?"

"Yes."

"Hell."

Raine nodded. "You took the word right out of my mouth."

He thrust a hand through his nearly dry hair, combing it back from his forehead. Hints of sun-ripened gold highlighted the underlying brown, setting off the intense darkness of his eyes. "It doesn't make sense that they'd choose us of all people. You must have some idea why they'd pull a stunt like this."

"No, I don't." She made the lie as adamant as possible. She'd already handed him the Cupid Committee. He didn't need to know anything more than that. No point in giving him additional ammunition to turn against her.

There was only one possible reason the committee would have set up this scenario, not that she'd admit as much to Lucien. It had to be related to the agreement she'd made with Tess and Emma. When the three of them had been in college they'd pledged to find each other the perfect husband, if they weren't married by the time they turned thirty. But that was years ago and they'd been joking around. And even though Tess had gone to the Cupid Committee on Emma's behalf when they'd all reached the big 3-0, that didn't mean that she'd done it for Raine, not when Raine had made it crystal clear that she wasn't the least interested in their assistance in that department. Besides, why would they choose Lucien, of all men?

"What?" Lucien demanded. "You've thought of something."

How did he keep doing that? She'd always thought she kept a good poker face. Apparently not, at least not when it came to Kincaid. "I have no idea why they'd think we'd make a good match," she maintained stubbornly. "The two of us had a brief fling—"

"A one-night stand," he cut in.

She mentally flinched from his statement, but nodded

equitably enough. No point in starting trouble when they were stuck here for the night with one stove, a single bed, and little to cover their assets other than a pair of sheets. "Fine," she managed to say in her most reasonable tone of voice. "We had a one-night stand when we were little more than kids. That still doesn't explain—"

His head jerked up. "Wait a minute. That's what your note said."

She broke off in confusion. "Excuse me?"

"Your note, dammit! The one I threw away. It referred to our being kids at the time of our—"

"Indiscretion," she inserted smoothly. "And your point is…?"

"You're using the exact same words that were in that message." He folded his arms across his chest and fixed her with a hard gaze. The stance struck her as both impressive and intimidating, possibly because the man taking up that stance was half naked and—for some reason—ticked as hell. "You mind explaining that?"

"I don't understand what I'm supposed to explain."

"You're using the same phrase that was in that message I received. That strikes me as quite a coincidence. And since I don't put much stock in coincidence, I'm thinking there might be another explanation."

"What are you suggesting?" Her breathing kicked up a notch as she made the connection. Did he really believe she was in cahoots with the Cupid Committee? Worse, that she considered him appealing husband material? "You big jerk!"

"Yup. That was in the note, too."

"All that proves is that someone else considers you as big a one as I do." She took her frustration out on the sheet. Somehow it kept sneaking underfoot in a dastardly attempt to trip her up. She gave the trailing ends

a good, swift kick. Not that it did much good. Finished
teasing her feet, now the blasted thing had decided to
imitate a boa constrictor and give her ankles a friendly
squeeze. She waddled to the nearest chair and sat down.
"Do you really think I have something to do with our
being here? Why? Because I used words similar to those
in the message you received?"

"It's more than that." His jawline assumed an aggressive slant. And why not? Attack was always the best
option, particularly when it came to a man as bullheaded
as Lucien. It didn't matter whether he stood on shaky
ground or, as in this case, thin air. When in doubt, start
pointing fingers until you run out of hands. "You must
have some of our communications left over from our last
round of warfare. That means you have access to my
handwriting. How tough would it be to imitate?"

"True." She unraveled the sheet from around her ankles. "All I'd have to do is dip some poor chicken in
ink and let it have at a stack of notepaper."

"You may notice I'm not laughing."

No, he wasn't. In fact, she'd guess he was holding on
to his temper by a thread. It wouldn't do to have both
of them lose it. Time to can the sarcasm and employ a
bit of calm reason. "Let me get this straight. You think
I sent you a note right before a major storm so we'd end
up stuck here. And I did it in order to force you into
some sort of matrimonial trap. That's the trail you're
following? You might notice it's leading you down a
loopy path." She added under her breath, "No surprise
there."

"I'm not following anything or anyone. I'm simply
asking a few innocent questions."

She straightened in the chair. No way would she let

him get away with that one. "Asking? How about accusing."

He inclined his head. "There might have been a bit of accusation thrown in there somewhere."

"Or more than a bit." She continued with her logical progression. "So after planning the storm and sending you a message calling you a jerk—the only part of this I can appreciate—"

"Watch it, Featherstone."

She laughed. "Don't get huffy with me. I mean... Damn, Kincaid. If all the provocation it takes to set you off on a wild-goose chase is to call you a jerk, you're going to waste most of your days chasing a flock of honkin' birds." She didn't give him a chance to do more than growl an insult that included her mother, her father, and a fair portion of her ancestors. "So after employing my most brilliant and devious methods of getting you to trot on out here—that's the highly successful 'calling you a jerk' ploy, in case you've forgotten—I then created another note, supposedly from you, written in handwriting identical to yours. That way when you accused me of dragging us up here, I can feign innocence because, hey-ho, I have a note, too. Is that how you're reading this?"

His brows drew together. "Maybe."

Her breath escaped just shy of a snort. "Or maybe not. Tell me why I would set you up? Why would I be the least bit interested in marrying you?"

"To get your hands on my land."

"I don't need to marry you to do that," she informed him. "As soon as I find the letter your grandfather wrote Nanna, I'll get it back fair and square."

"Not a chance. There is no letter."

A childish "is, too" hovered on her lips, one she ruthlessly suppressed. No point in starting a petty squabble. Time would prove him wrong soon enough. "We're getting off track, Lucien. Do you really think I'd go to such ridiculous lengths just to snare you in some crazy marriage trap? How? Let's say I wrote the notes and somehow got you out here. What next? How do I convince you to marry me? I suppose I could put a shotgun to your back and demand we chase down the nearest preacher. Marry me, or I blow you to kingdom come." She snapped her fingers. "No, gosh darn it. That won't work. Here I went to all that trouble to tempt you to my lair and I forgot the fool shotgun."

He rubbed his hand across the nape of his neck. "Aw, hell. That sounds crazy, even to me."

"Thank you."

"You really didn't have anything to do with this?"

"For the last time, no. I'm a victim, too. But I guarantee that when I find out who is responsible, I'm gonna tear a strip off their hide." And then some.

"I wouldn't mind a piece of that action. Only when I get through with them, they'll be missing more than a strip."

Raine never thought she and Lucien would be in accord about anything ever again. It was an odd sensation, one she wasn't certain she liked. Working in concert meant becoming far too close and personal and she didn't dare open that door again. Last time had caused untold pain, something to be avoided at all costs. Caution urged her to maintain a judicious distance on this go-round. Perhaps changing the tenor of their conversation to a safe and nonthreatening topic would be a smart move.

"Are you hungry?" she asked. "How about I rustle us up some grub?"

"Sounds good to me." Lucien crossed to one of the cupboards and flung the doors wide, examining the stack of tins it contained. "We have beans, beans, or beans."

"That's way too many choices. You decide."

He removed two cans. "Beans it is."

They spent the next half hour working side-by-side throwing together an edible meal. Even dinner passed companionably enough. Lucien didn't broach the subject of how they'd come to find themselves in their current predicament and Raine refrained from teasing him about any sensitive subjects. They also avoided mention of their respective properties, their workday, and any discussion related to family. Despite having so many taboo topics, they found plenty to talk about, the conversation never lagging.

By the time Raine was ready to call it a night the thunder and lightning had long since passed. Even the rain had slackened to a pathetic drizzle. All that remained was a constant tinny drip as rainwater splashed from the widespread branches of the elm onto the roof and from the roof into the bucket she'd placed beneath the eaves. With luck, the sheer monotony of the sound would knock her out cold.

"Care to flip for the bed?" she offered.

"Nah. You take it." Lucien removed the blanket from the line and spread it into a simple bedroll near the stove. "I've slept under worse conditions."

"You were a lot younger then," she dared to joke, retreating to the bed.

He settled onto the blanket, folding his arms behind his head. "Like you have room to talk. Wasn't your last birthday one of those major milestones?"

"Milestones or millstones?"

He didn't tease back, which surprised her. Instead his

tone turned serious. "Has hitting thirty been a millstone?"

She curled up on the mattress. "It's not so bad, I suppose."

"Is it also not so good?" When she didn't immediately answer, he asked, "Is the bad part because you don't have a husband or kids?"

"Nope," she lied cheerfully. If he ever guessed she was out trolling for a husband, she'd never hear the end of it. Nor would she be able to curb his suspicions about her involvement in today's events. "How about you? Do you have a hankering for a wife and a corral full of little ones?"

"Not a chance. No way, no how."

Did he have to sound so adamant? "Glad we got that cleared up." With luck the finality in her voice would bring a fast end to an uncomfortable conversation. "What do you say we catch some shut-eye?"

He must have decided they'd pursued the discussion further than they should have, because he doused the kerosene lamps. "Sounds good to me."

Settling the sheet more comfortably around her, she closed her eyes. She'd half expected her awareness of Lucien to keep her awake. But that didn't prove to be the case. Within minutes consciousness faded.

It wasn't until hours later that she came to. It took a minute to realize what had woken her. Turning over, she stared at the ceiling. It was raining again, the tin roof magnifying the intense pounding. How did the men who used the line shack stand it? Maybe over time they grew accustomed to the noise. Or maybe their snores drowned out the sound.

"You awake?" Lucien asked in a sleep-roughened voice.

"It's a little tough snoozing through all that racket."

"We really are getting old if we can't handle the pitter pat of a little rain." He yawned. "Since sleeping's out, how 'bout you give me more information on this Cupid Committee."

"Okay." At some point during the night the sheet had become wound around her waist. Unwrapping it, she shook it out and folded it loosely around herself. "What do you want to know?"

"Let's start with how this outfit operates."

She considered how much to reveal. Might as well be completely frank. Knowing Lucien, he'd get the information one way or another. "The best I can figure, the committee works behind the scenes sparking romances."

"How do they decide who to put together?"

The bedsprings squeaked as she rolled over to face him. She could just make out his outline from the bit of light the stove threw off. A reddish-gold glow reflected off the powerful definition of shoulders and chest before sinking into shadowy crevices that begged a more tactile exploration. She buried her face in her arms. Maybe if she didn't look, she wouldn't be tempted to touch.

"I guess they're approached by friends and family who have someone they'd like matched," came her muffled response.

"What happens after that?"

"They have these Inciters…" No. That wasn't right. What was Shadoe's title? "Instigators. They have Instigators who take over from there."

"I gather they're the actual cupids?"

"Right. The cupids manipulate events so the two people being matched are thrown together."

"Like now."

"Yeah. Like now. Not that it's working." She peeked at him from beneath her arms. "Right?"

"Not a lick," he insisted a little too adamantly.

She closed her eyes. Tight. "Didn't think so."

He paused and she knew he was busy thinking through the problem. Or was he fighting to keep those licks at bay? "What happens if nothing comes of this Instigator's matchmaking attempts?"

"I'm not sure." She frowned. It was a good question. What did happen? She couldn't believe they simply gave up. "I don't know much about them, Kincaid. Just what Tess told me and that was darn little."

"But someone has to actually approach them and make a request?"

Where was he going with this? "I assume so."

"That means someone we know paid them a visit."

She hadn't thought of that. "Who? No one I know even likes you."

"Same here."

"Then it has to be someone who hates us enough to want to stick us in an impossible marriage."

"Must have seriously ticked someone off," Lucien said morosely. "Wish I knew who."

She couldn't help it. She started to laugh. "Listen to us. One of our friends or relatives probably thinks they're doing us a favor by marrying us off to each other and we act as if we're being tortured."

"Tortured? Hell, sweetheart, marriage to you would be—"

His voice broke off and her laughter faded. "Marriage to me would be what?"

The rain chose that minute to kick up, drowning out his reply. She could have sworn he'd said "heaven." But she must have misunderstood him. There wasn't any other explanation. He'd actually said "akin to hades" and she heard it wrong. She sat up in the bed. "Lucien?"

"If you're real smart, you'll stay put," he ordered gruffly.

She clasped the sheet to her chest. "Did you say heaven?"

"Aw, hell." His breath escaped in a rough sigh. "I might have said something to that effect."

"Why would it be heaven?" she asked in bewilderment. "I thought we hated each other."

He was silent for a long moment. "You know why." The words sounded as if they'd been torn from him. "You remember how it was between us. What else would you call it?"

"Sex."

"No way, sweetheart. I've had sex and that wasn't it."

She cautiously planted her big toe on the cold wooden floor. "Then what was it?"

"You move another muscle off that mattress and you'll find out."

"Okay."

But whether she meant "okay" she intended to move a whole body full of muscles or "okay" she wouldn't be budging anytime in the next millennium, she never found out. A loud squeal ripped through the cabin. It was followed by a series of ear-splitting pops before the world crashed down on her.

"Lucien!" she screamed.

And then darkness descended.

"Raine!"

It took Lucien a minute to determine where he was and what had happened to him. The tree. The tree had fallen on the cabin. All that rain must have loosened the elm's grip on the hillside and sent it tumbling into the river, taking the line shack along for the ride. The best he could tell, he lay in the only portion of the cabin still intact. Where once a roof had protected him from the elements, now open sky canopied his position.

He shoved at the tent of timber piled over him and sat up, looking around. The rain had slackened off and just enough light filtered through the thinning clouds for him to get his bearings. The side of the cabin with the wood-burning stove was completely gone. At a guess, it had plummeted down the hillside into the river. And a damn good thing, too, or he'd be fighting a fire along with everything else. He could hear the rush and roar of water in full flood uncomfortably nearby. It wouldn't be long before the river ate what remained of the shack. He and Raine had to get out of here. Now.

Raine! He fought back a wave of sheer terror. Where was she?

He scrambled up the listing floorboards toward where the bed had been. Snapped branches from the fallen elm stabbed through what remained of the caved-in roof. If he'd been the imaginative sort, he'd have likened it to a great prehistoric beast locking its jaws around the cabin, crushing it between stakelike wooden teeth.

"Raine! Where are you, sweetheart?"

To his intense relief, she answered, though he could barely hear her. "Lucien? I'm stuck!"

"Are you hurt?" he shouted.

"I don't think so. But I'm trapped." Her muffled voice came to him from a distance, off to his left and beneath him toward what had been the back of the cabin. "There's something on top of me."

Planks and strips of roofing tin blocked his access to her. "Hang on." He tossed the rubble aside with more urgency than care. "I'm coming."

Maybe. It wasn't just the collapsed wreck of the cabin impeding him. Thick branches also barred his path and they wouldn't be as easily shifted. Planting his back against a section of the downed tree trunk, he braced his foot against the first of the branches and used brute force to shove it aside. His sole skittered along the branch gathering up splinters and he swore furiously that he had neither boots nor gloves for protection. Hell, he didn't even have clothes, other than this blasted sheet. With a tremendous groan, the branch finally gave, allowing him passage.

Squeezing past the thicker limbs, Lucien battled his way into a thicket of whip thin branches covered in leaves still drenched from the storm. He paused long enough to catch his breath, wiping sweat-soaked hair from his eyes. What he wouldn't give for a good sharp machete. He'd have hacked apart this briar patch with a few quick swipes. Instead, he was reduced to wriggling along like a snake shedding a skin two sizes too tight.

"Lucien?" Music rippled through her use of his name. The fact that she'd resorted to using her "touch" warned that even though she sounded calm, fear wasn't far off. "Are you still there?"

"I'm closing in." He snatched a quick breath and straightened. "It won't be much longer."

"I wish I'd brought Dog. He could have led you to me."

"I'll find you even without Dog. I promise."

Confronting the next section he needed to tackle, he calculated the best way past the clutter of crushed cabin and uprooted tree. By the time he'd wrested a path through, he was soaked, covered in tree debris, and had accumulated a fair share of assorted cuts, bruises and scratches. Hell's bells. Crawling naked through a cactus patch couldn't be worse than this.

"Talk to me, hon. Where are you?"

"Down here." Her voice came from his left, still muffled, but within reach. "I can't see. I can't move."

And it terrified her, he could tell. "I'll have you out in a tick. I'm almost there."

The moon broke through the roiling clouds once again, spotlighting his position. Part of the bed stood between him and his goal, the metal frame crumpled beneath a huge fallen branch. He flinched from the sight. Raine could have been under that. How she'd escaped could only be thanks to divine intervention.

Somehow he had to get beneath the remains of both the tree and cabin. The tough part was…this section of the cabin didn't look any too secure. He climbed gingerly downward, past a strange assortment of odds and ends. Part of the clothesline had snagged here, but no clothing. Naturally. It would have been too much to hope that he could find a pair of jeans or even so much as a sock. A cup dangled from a twig hook, and an assortment of canned goods were scattered across the thick foliage like bizarre Christmas tree bulbs. And of all things, he found the frying pan that had contained their dinner hanging drunkenly off a splintered branch.

Lucien removed it from its precarious perch and tossed it out of the way. Easing aside a crumpled portion of the roof, an opening appeared beneath him and he realized that this section of the cabin had collapsed over the roots of the tree. He wedged into the narrow hole, dropping down to a good-size cave of soft dirt and scrub grass.

"Raine? Where are you, sweetheart?"

"This way."

Lucien remained crouched near the hole, taking a moment to assess the situation while his eyesight adjusted to the gloom. Raine must have fallen through the broken floorboards, the mattress landing on top of her. One of the half-snapped roots stabbed into the center of the mattress, pinning her to the earth beneath. He examined it carefully to make sure that breaking off this section of the tree wouldn't meet with catastrophic results. Satisfied that disaster wasn't imminent, he grasped the mud-encrusted root with his good hand and ripped it free.

Upending the mattress, he uncovered Raine. A lazy grin eased the corners of his mouth. "Hey, there, lady."

Her grin was as big as his. "Hey, yourself."

She lay on her back, her hair spilling across the rich loam in earthy abandon, the sheet spread open beneath her. She drew in a deep breath of fresh air, drawing his attention to the few scraps of silk that were her only covering. That answered one of his questions. The cotton undergarments had gone by the wayside, after all. He couldn't tell if she'd chosen to wear the red he'd imagined her in, but it was possible. The tiny triangles were dark shadows against her paler skin, like tiny hands modestly concealing her more feminine aspects.

"Hang on and let's make sure nothing's broken." He kept his touch brisk and impersonal, careful never to linger or caress, despite his druthers. "I'm not finding anything obvious. How do you feel?"

"Sore. Scared."

"Could have been a hell of a lot worse." Leaning forward, he gently folded the edges of the sheet over her and helped her sit up. A smudge decorated one cheek and he attempted to erase it with his thumb. He only succeeded in making it worse, possibly because his hand was every bit as dirty as her cheek. "Best I can tell the tree let loose thanks to all that wind and rain."

"Anything left of the cabin?"

"Damn little."

She swept his shoulders with her fingertips. "How about you? Are you hurt?"

Her touch provoked thoughts inappropriate to the situation. But they existed, nonetheless, teasing at his senses and tempting him beyond endurance. They were primitive thoughts, and even more primitive emotions, urging him to push her back against the rich earth and celebrate their survival in a manner as old as time.

"Lucien?"

He shook his head, fighting to remember what she'd asked. Something about being hurt. Taking a deep breath, he managed to keep his tone light and easy. "Well, now. I have to admit that I've had a tough half hour working my backside off to rescue a damsel in distress. Other than that, I'm fine."

She responded to his teasing by relaxing against him. "Really? And here I've been lying around catching up on my beauty sleep instead of lending a hand."

He released a frustrated laugh. Now she chose to get affectionate, when he didn't dare pursue the opportunity. "You all caught up now?"

"Sure am. How about we get the hell out of here?"

"My thoughts, exactly." Reluctantly leaving her side, he crept in a back-breaking crouch toward the opening. "Let me go first. As soon as I'm sure it's safe, I'll give you a shout."

"Be careful."

"Count on it."

He jumped for a thick length of branch hanging just

above the narrow opening and caught hold of it with both hands. Pain ripped from elbow to fingertip along his injured arm. With one bum wrist, this was going to hurt. Taking a deep breath, he did a slow chin-up, dragging himself cautiously up through the hole. He'd gotten halfway through when he heard an ominous crack. Raine must have heard it, as well.

"Lucien!" she shouted. "Get back."

With an ear-splitting squeal, the branches of the elm overhead shuddered, collapsing inward. He didn't hesitate. Releasing his hold, he dropped straight back through the hole in a desperate free-fall. He hit the ground hard, rolling away from the opening just as half the tree and the remains of the cabin crashed down after him. He heard Raine shout his name, the tone as much an order as an entreaty. It gave him the extra impetus he needed. Digging his feet into the dirt, he pushed backward, scrambling to escape the cascading debris with all body parts intact. The screech of collapsing timber continued for an endless minute, the sound shrill and painful. Dust and dirt exploded around them in a choking cloud.

And then it stopped.

Darkness descended, along with a brief, eerie silence.

CHAPTER FOUR

THE silence was broken an instant later from somewhere behind him. "Lucien." Raine wept beneath her breath. "Oh, please. Lucien, say something."

"Something."

It must not have been the something she was looking for. She burst into great racking sobs. Lucien winced. Okay, smartass. Lesson learned. Next time he found himself trapped in a line shack with Raine in the middle of a thunderstorm and the damned thing collapsed under a tree and Raine asked him to say something, he wasn't supposed to take her literally. "Something" meant any word other than that one. He crawled toward her.

"I'm sorry, honey. I didn't mean to upset you." A rock stabbed him in the side. He took it stoically, biting back a few choice words. Dragging his sorry self over a pile of rocks was a small price to pay for scaring her. A little pain served him right. Or even a lot of pain. "I'm okay. Honest."

She threw herself in his direction, knocking him back onto the rock he'd just climbed off of. This time he couldn't suppress a groan. "What?" she demanded. "What's wrong?"

"Nothing."

Apparently, "nothing" ranked right up there with "something." More tears flowed. "Don't give me that," she managed to argue. "You're hurt. I can hear it in your voice."

"That's a switch," he muttered. "I thought you were the one with the voice."

Her hands swept across his shoulders and down his arms. She must not have discovered anything gruesome enough to warrant further investigation because she splayed her fingers across his chest, sinking into the crisp hair spanning his breastbone. She traced a tantalizing path downward, stopping just shy of the end of the trail. Or perhaps it was the remains of his sheet that slowed her. It rode low on his hips, threatening an eager parting of the ways.

To his intense disappointment, her hands didn't investigate further, instead fluttering to his face in order to relearn the aggressive slant of his jawline. Next she traced the slight crick centered atop his nose, the one he'd earned in that long-ago barroom brawl defending her honor, before finally shifting out toward the flare of his cheekbones.

He returned the favor. Cupping her face, he swept away her tears. They clung to his battered hands, affecting him on some inexplicable level. Or perhaps they'd infected him, filling his blood with a potent toxin that caused his brain to shut down and sheer animal drive to take over. He drew her closer, awkwardly seeking her mouth in the darkness. Her breath escaped in a surprised rush, filling the silence of their earthen cave. He honed in, capturing her parted lips beneath his.

He didn't bother with preliminaries. He consumed her softness, invaded the readily parted barrier of her lips until he gained the inner sanctum. She was warm and sweet and just as eager. They dueled for supremacy, locked in a give-and-take that stopped time in its tracks. Their breath escaped in quick, hungry gasps and in between kisses she bit out a frantic demand. Or did it come from him? He didn't know or care. All that mattered was that he keep kissing her. Touching her. That he find a way to forge a bond between them more powerful than wind, or rain, or raging river.

He reached behind her, feeling around until he hit on the mattress he'd pulled off her. They tumbled onto it in a desperate jumble of damp sheets and slick arms and entwined legs. He rolled beneath her, never once breaking the seal of their mouths. The tangled rope of her hair bound them close, chaining them as one.

"Easy," he murmured. "Easy, honey. We're going to be fine. You'll see."

She dropped a flurry of kisses across his jaw. His shoulders. His chest. "I thought you'd been killed."

The sweetness of each caress pulled the bitter ache from his bruises and he released his breath on a sigh of sheer pleasure. "Takes more than dropping a shack on my head to do me in."

"You forgot about the tree."

"Yeah, that caused me a moment or two of worry."

As though in response to their levity, the remains of the cabin shifted again, coughing out an ominous rumble. His reaction came with instinctive swiftness. He rolled across the mattress, sweeping her beneath him, bracing himself above her in order to absorb any potential impact. Raine wrapped her arms around him, burying her head against his shoulder.

"Don't," she pleaded. "Don't risk yourself again. Not for me."

He smoothed her hair back from her face, striving to keep his voice light and teasing. "Pure reflex, ma'am. If I stopped to think about it, I'd have hid behind you." He reared back slightly, poking at her arm. "Though I doubt it would have done much good considering how puny you are.''

A tearful laugh escaped. ''Liar. You'd never hide behind a woman. And I'm not puny.''

''Nah. Not puny. Lean and lanky, yet lush in all the most interesting places.''

The collapsing cabin released a final death rattle and Lucien continued to follow his instincts, though these were far different from before. This instinct drove him to give Raine something more crucial to think about than their close call. This instinct drove him to commit the most natural act in the world.

Closing his mouth over hers once again, he yanked at the edges of her sheet, parting them. He couldn't see very well. The dark was intense, as much a depravation of sound and sensation as it was sight. The only other person who existed within the darkness was Raine. Nature's nighttime symphony was silenced and all he could hear was the ardent catch of her breath. All he could feel was the exquisite softness of her body. All he could smell and taste was her unique essence. It heightened his desire to an almost painful level.

She must have felt the same for she called to him, using her siren's voice to lure him closer, to enchant and bind him on some intangible level, as thoroughly as her hair tethered them together physically. A ferocious need gripped him. He hadn't felt its like in years. Not since the last time he'd made love to Raine.

The only time he'd made love to Raine.

It returned full force now, reminding him of what he'd spent years trying to forget. She was bewitching. Joining with her had been an occurrence beyond explanation or logical understanding, while losing her had just about crippled him, killing some vital part of him that he'd never even known existed until he and Raine had parted. He wanted to experience that feeling again, to share that special touch of magic.

"Stop me now," he warned. "Because I won't be able to in another minute."

"I'm not stopping you. I couldn't."

"You'll regret this come morning. Hell, I'll regret it."

"It's not morning, is it?"

No it wasn't. He'd held himself in check as long as possible. The urgency returned, a determination to defy the fates and celebrate their survival. Reaching behind her, he unhitched her bra, stripping it from her. Her panties followed close behind, sliding down the shapeliest legs in half a dozen counties. Maybe in all of Texas.

"I wish I could see you."

"You can." She cradled his hands in hers and guided them to her body. "Touch me and remember."

He spanned the narrow indent at her waist while a roaring grew in his ears, a roaring that had nothing to do with storms or fallen cabins or twisting timber. "My hands are dirty," he protested thickly.

"So are mine." A soft laugh brushed his face. "Guess this time we'll leave tracks behind."

An image of her covered with handprints filled his mind. His handprints. Marks of his possession. "Raine," he groaned.

"Have you closed your eyes, yet?"

Driven to do as she asked, he shut his eyes. "They're closed."

"Remember last time? You lit up the cabin with oil lamps."

"They turned your skin to gold."

They'd moved the mattress to the center of the room and covered it with cotton sheets that were far too fine

and soft for his weather-roughened skin. They were
white sheets. Virginal sheets more appropriate for a
bride than a momentary expression of youthful passion.
Those sheets had given him pause. But only until she'd
stood and calmly removed her clothing.

There'd been something elemental about what she'd
done. Something natural and right. Her serenity and as-
surance had overridden his hesitation and in that instant,
they belonged together as surely as if they'd stood before
a preacher and spoken vows. Their love felt deep and
certain and eternal.

It was only later that it had all fallen apart.

Lucien shook his head to clear the thought, focusing
on how she'd looked with lamplight casting a soft glow
across her naked skin. Her hair had been like a sheet of
black silk cascading down her back to wrap around her
golden flanks. Then she'd walked to the center of their
makeshift bed and laid down in the center of all that
whiteness. He'd never witnessed anything more erotic or
arousing.

"You were perfection," he whispered.

"So were you. I haven't seen the like before or
since."

The confession nearly proved his undoing. He slid his
hands from her waist, tracing upward to her breasts. He
remembered them so clearly. Their silken weight. The
dusky, pearled crests. The taste of them in his mouth.
With a groan, he lowered his head, making the vision a
reality.

Her breath exploded from her lungs at the first hungry
swipe of his tongue and she arched beneath him. He
teased the rigid tip. Tugged at it. Fanned it repeatedly
with mouth and teeth and tongue. Sinking her fingers
deep into his hair, she held him tight within her embrace.

It wasn't enough. He wanted more from her. Far more. That long-ago night when he'd first made her his had been the most memorable of his life and he intended to experience those sensations again. He wanted to hear her sing, wanted the music to spill from her voice and drive them toward an enchantment beyond anything he'd ever experienced with any other woman.

He slid a hand between their bodies, seeking the moist delta at the apex of her legs. She shifted to accommodate him and he stroked upward along the silk of her inner thigh. He paused just shy of his goal, allowing her to make the decision of where they went from here. Parting her knees, she opened to him in an invitation as old as time. He didn't hesitate. He warmed his hand in her feminine heat and eased his fingers through the soft curls to the very heart of her. His thumb found the core of her desire and brushed it with a feather-light caress. A shudder trembled through her and a needy hum built in her throat.

It still wasn't enough. He wanted more. He wanted the magic.

Again he brushed her with his thumb. Once. Twice. And then a third slow circle.

"Lucien!"

Her voice rose in demand, filling their secret cave, overflowing it, lashing at them with all the energy of nature unbridled. Yes! This was what he'd waited to hear. This was the sound that vibrated deep within, shattering him with a spectacular combination of unworldly strength and earthly desire. His voice coupled with hers in an intensely masculine response, a demand to accept what he was driven to give. To take him within her, sheathe him, absorb his power and combine it with her own. To transpose it—as only a woman could—into

something more than a mere mating. To make it the
irrevocable and life-altering joining that forever changed
man and woman. He moved on her, long past any
attempt at a slow seduction. Goaded by pure arousal,
finesse deserted him. A single impetus rode him.

To make her his.

Palming her bottom, he lifted her to him, penetrating
her in one smooth stroke. He threw back his head, his
throat moving convulsively. For a long moment, he
couldn't continue, could only wallow in pure sensation.
The tightness. The heat. The slick softness. The desperate urge to mate competed with his need for restraint
and he literally shook from the effort to hold back and
make this moment right for both of them. To impose
some semblance of control over a more imperative instinct.

She captured his face in her hands, drawing him to
her. "Let go," she ordered.

The command ripped through the air, impacting with
all the force of a shotgun blast. As the words faded, so
did his control. With a bull-like roar, he did as she asked.
He let go of all pretense that he could govern what was
happening between them. He couldn't change the direction of where this took them any more than he could the
direction of the storm that had placed them here.

He slid into her again and again, the rhythmic motion
becoming a pounding, the pounding a savage grinding
of male into female. A dark lust. A beautiful desire. A
painful need. An ecstasy beyond compare. She met him
thrust for thrust, calling to him with her siren's voice,
compelling him to greater heights. And then the music
came, torn from her throat. It washed over him. Filled
him. Cleansed him. Colors exploded behind his eyelids,
ripped him apart body and soul.

With a hoarse shout, he drove home. Beneath him Raine sang out her own climax, the sound a rich expression of pure rapture. He held her close, absorbing the feminine tremors with a bone-deep satisfaction. So, the last time they'd come together hadn't been a one-off occurrence. Somehow, in some inexplicable way, their joining sparked a reaction that went beyond simple explanation or understanding. He wallowed in the pleasure of that knowledge, taking her mouth in a final biting kiss, one she returned with unmistakable urgency. She clung to him, as though to defy what fate had in store for them as a result of their transgression.

Gradually the sounds of their passion faded until all that remained was the urgent give and take of their combined breath. Finally, even that slowed. He held her for those last bittersweet minutes, absorbing her into his skin even as he stamped her with his very essence.

And then, sanity returned.

What had she done?

Raine fought to control her breathing. But it was too soon for anything resembling control. The aftermath of their lovemaking continued to ripple through her in great waves of delicious warmth. She didn't want the moment to end, didn't want sanity to return. Because then she'd have to deal with the consequences of her actions.

Lucien continued to cover her, still possessing her even after their passion had been spent. His scent invaded her, overwhelmed her. It was a part of her, as familiar as his touch and voice and taste. Years ago he'd branded her with his possession and now she felt that brand again, the sensation going deeper, growing more intense than before. It connected them on every possible level.

Did he feel it, too? Did she affect him the same way? She must. What had he said about the last time they'd been together? *I've had sex and that wasn't it.* Despite their differences, despite everything that kept them apart, there was a connection that wouldn't be denied. Only one question remained....

What the hell were they going to do about it?

"Are you all right?" His voice rumbled close to her ear. He eased back slightly, bracing his elbows on either side of her head. "Did I hurt you?"

She could end things right now. All she had to do was push him away and offer a cool, "Hey, thanks" and the moment would be shattered. He might be offended, but she'd have protected herself from a world of future hurt. She started to do just that. But somehow she found the sweep of his jaw instead of his chest. Sliding her hands along the raspy surface, her fingers sank deep into his hair.

"No," she murmured gently, pulling him down for a leisurely kiss. "You didn't hurt me."

"Regrets?"

"They'll come soon enough, I'm afraid, but right now I can't work up the energy."

He rolled off her. Scooping her close, he clasped her body tight against his. She'd forgotten what it was like to lay naked in a man's arms, to feel the intense dichotomy of masculine and feminine. They were polar opposites, as different from each other as the earth from the moon. And yet just like those heavenly bodies, they were locked together in a dance of sweet perfection, neither complete without the other.

Lucien broke the silence with a gusty sigh. "Yup."

She lifted her head from his shoulder. "Yup, what?"

"When I started out this morning I had it all planned."

Uh-oh. "What did you have planned?"

"I'd planned to drop by this old line shack. Then I planned to get myself stranded with the woman associated with one of my best memories. Next up on the list was to ride out the storm from hell with her. Have a tree eat the cabin and us along with it. Screw up my first ever attempt to play knight errant to her damsel in distress. And finally, I scribbled myself a note to make love like there was no tomorrow." He rested his chin against the top of her head. "Isn't that how you planned your day when you got up this morning?"

She imitated his slow drawl. "Yup."

"Thought you might have." He waited a beat. "What are your plans for tomorrow? Anything like today?"

Like today? She swiftly assessed the question, attempting to read the underlying meaning. He couldn't be asking what she imagined, could he? "I think I'll try for something a little quieter," she offered tentatively.

"Quieter, huh? I guess that means I won't be getting any more messages to meet you at deserted line shacks?"

More messages? She lay there, stunned. There wasn't anything subtle about that question. No underlying meaning. Nothing to analyze. He'd put the offer right out there for her to accept or reject. She struggled to get her heartbeat under control as she considered her options. It hadn't occurred to her that they could do this on a regular basis. Well... Parts of it, anyway. The parts worth repeating—not the parts with trees crashing down and cabins collapsing and getting trapped under the ruins.

The prospect of making love to Lucien again opened

a whole new world of possibilities and she allowed herself to contemplate them for a few blissful moments.
They could actually plan a romantic rendezvous, instead
of it just happening to them. Heck, they were grown-
ups. In fact, at thirty and thirty-three, respectively, they
could be considered by some less charitable folk as sliding down the wrong side of a slippery slope, headed
straight toward a serious case of old age. One plus to
that was that old people were allowed to behave odd. It
was expected of them.

Good heavens! She and Lucien could behave odd on
a frequent basis. Heck, they could ride up to whichever
line shack appealed, throw their clothing to the four
winds, and indulge in all sorts of odd behavior without
any of the pain and destruction that had highlighted tonight's episode. Best of all, they could do it without the
accompanying dirt and grime.

Now that she thoroughly considered the matter, they
could sample every single line shack on Kincaid and
Featherstone property. How long would that take? Depending on the enthusiasm with which they tackled the
project, probably not long enough. Still, once they'd
tried each one, they could revisit some of their all-time
favorites. So long as they didn't leave any of them in a
state of disrepair similar to this one, nobody would ever
be the wiser.

The possibility of more nights like tonight made her
dizzy with excitement. This could be so incredible. Only
one question remained. Did Lucien share her opinion or
had he been throwing out a lure just to see if anyone
was hungry enough to bite?

She approached the discussion on tiptoe. "I don't
think meeting again would be smart. What's your opin-

ion on the matter?'' Somehow a hint of hopefulness had climbed into her words.

"It would be downright foolhardy. We're grown adults, not a couple of randy kids.'' His voice dropped to a soft rumble. "But would you do it?''

In a heartbeat. "I suspect the temptation would be almost more than I could bear,'' she confessed.

"Yeah. That's sort of how I feel, too.''

Right up until someone caught on to what they were doing, came the sobering thought.

And someone always caught on.

An image of Nanna's reaction came to her and Raine winced. Nanna didn't believe in an excess of passion outside of marriage. One transgression was understandable, expected even. But a second, and at Raine's age, invited a serious talking to. And Nanna could talk like no one Raine had ever met before. It wasn't just that she had the "gift.'' It went deeper than that. Nanna had strong views on right and wrong, views Raine had absorbed over their lifetime together.

If she and Lucien decided to have a fling, they'd be doing it beneath a cloud of serious Nanna guilt. As obstinate as Lucien had frequently proven himself to be, even he couldn't stand up to that. Well, heck. When she balanced the unbelievable pleasure of misbehaving with the resulting consequences, all that guilt sort of sapped the fun right out of it.

"We can't,'' she stated. Excellent. She sounded absolute. Uncompromising. No room for talking her into something she desperately wanted to do.

"Nanna?''

Raine sighed. "Nanna.''

"She going to hang me for tonight?''

"If she does, I'll be dangling at the end of a rope, right alongside of you."

"Somehow I think she'd forgive and forget this one slip," he offered.

"But not another."

"No."

He was silent for a long time. And then he said in a far too casual voice, "There could be consequences from tonight, you know."

Her brain chose that moment to lock up on her. "Consequences?" she repeated stupidly.

"Of the nine-month variety."

She fought for breath. No. How could she have forgotten something as basic as that? "You mean... A baby?"

"That's often the result when we've been doing what the two of us have, without using what we weren't." He rested his palm low on her belly, the touch both possessive and questing—as though he were feeling for the start of a new life. "Unless you're on the pill?"

"No."

"Sorta figured that would be your answer." His fingers splayed outward, brushing the soft curls between her thighs. "You need to take one of those tests as soon as possible."

His touch made it hard to concentrate, though the subject matter kept her from completely losing it. "And if I'm pregnant?" she asked unevenly.

"We'll deal with the ifs once they become fer sures."

"I didn't plan this." The comment exploded from her. "Not a lick of it."

"Well, no," he agreed reasonably enough. "I can see you didn't, or you would have taken precautions."

"No, I mean, this isn't some devious plot to get Nanna's land back."

He paused long enough to consider the possibility. "I have to admit, there'd be easier ways of going about it."

"I just wanted to make that clear. What happened was—"

"Be careful what you say."

He'd lost her again. "About what?"

"This is a memory I intend to hold on to for a long, long time. When I'm an old man and the spring's gone from my step, this memory will keep the twinkle in my eyes. And I won't have that memory tarnished before it even becomes one. When I'm rocking away on my front porch, I want people wondering what the hell such an old geezer has to smile about."

"You're going to smile about this?" She wasn't quite sure, but she suspected she should be insulted. "Something about what happened amuses you?"

"No. Something about what happened will stay with me for the rest of my life." An edginess drifted through his words. "Won't it stay with you?"

If a baby resulted, it would definitely stay with her. Then she closed her eyes, accepting the bittersweet truth. Whether she conceived a child or not, this night would always remain one of the most special she'd ever experienced. How could it not? It ranked right up there with the other occasion she'd made love with Lucien. Revisiting that night often proved painful. But it was also a moment of incandescent brightness.

This experience would prove the same. If their circumstances had been different, they might have explored a relationship. Perhaps it would have developed into something serious, something that would have matured and deepened into more than a simple twinkle in an old man's eyes. A painful longing filled her and she inched closer to Lucien, drawing comfort from his warmth. She intended to savor every second of what time remained, because that's all she'd ever have—this fleeting moment that fate had bestowed.

"Yes, tonight will stay with me," she whispered.

It would stay with her forever.

He should be upset. He should be fighting tooth and nail to find a way out of their situation.

Lucien traced the length of Raine's spine, filling the hollow above her buttocks with his hand. He sure shouldn't be enjoying their predicament. And he sure as hell shouldn't be chock-full of such blatant complacency. They were risking serious consequences here.

A baby.

Damn. Hadn't he just told her a few short hours ago that he didn't have a hankering for either a wife or a corral full of little ones? He still didn't. No way, no how.

But what if she were pregnant?

An image of Raine with a babe at her breast leapt to mind, threatening to unman him. Even as he relaxed in the afterglow of the most incredible lovemaking he'd experienced in many a year, things could be happening. What if, now that his compatriots had finally escaped the rubber room that normally contained them, they were busily whooping it up over having roped themselves a fertile filly? While he lay here, exhausted from having given his all, two to four hundred million of his eager and energetic buddies could be duking it out over who'd be the first to saddle and ride her.

For some reason he found it hard to breathe.

What were the odds that one of them wouldn't succeed? Hell, he was a pretty determined kind of guy. No doubt all his various parts and byproducts were every bit as determined. Four hundred million to one. Maybe five or six hundred million, because sure as shootin' he'd be on the high end of the average. Big hands, big feet, it made sense he'd also have an extra heapin' helping of little buddies. A knot kinked his innards. With those sort of odds, Raine's own little friend didn't stand a chance. The pressure built until he couldn't stand it another second.

He bolted upright.

"Turn around, girl!" he shouted. "Head back upstream before it's too late!"

Raine leapt into a catlike crouch.

"What? What's wrong?"

Beside her, Lucien dragged air into his lungs as though he were on the verge of suffocation. "Sorry," he gasped. "Guess I was dreaming."

"Sounds more like a nightmare to me."

"Yeah. A nightmare." He thrust a hand through his hair, his breath still coming in deep, sharp gasps. "All my buddies were closing in and the only way out was to make a run for it."

Okaaaay. She grazed his shoulder, feeling a slight dampness between his shoulder blades. "Do you think our being trapped here has made you a little claustrophobic?"

"I'm not claustrophobic," he instantly denied. "Leastwise, I wasn't until the crowd closed in."

Her brow crinkled. "A crowd of your buddies? Is that what you said?"

"Yeah, lots and lots of buddies. Stands to reason I'd have a touch of trouble, what with everyone pushing to get to the front of the line."

"Uh-huh." His breathing had slackened off, though she could still feel his heart thundering against her palm. "Something good at the front of that line?"

"Guess that depends on your perspective," he answered cautiously.

"Got it." She deliberately infused a dollop of sympathy into her comment, hoping it would calm him. "Whoopee if you're at the front of the pack and not-so whoopee if you're at the back. I understand."

He flinched. "Do you think you could pick a different word than whoopee?"

"Yahoo? Bingo?" She snapped her fingers. "How about whiz-bang?"

"Whiz-bang? What, are you nuts?" He lay back on the mattress again and dragged her down beside him. "Now listen up and listen good, Featherstone. No whiz-banging. Anything but that. Got it?"

No. "Sure, Lucien. I got it."

"You've got a peculiar tone in your voice," he growled. "You using that gift of your yours again?"

"I thought it might help you sleep."

"Well, cut it out. Odd things happen when you use it. We can't afford to have you woo-woo anything else into happening."

"Woo-woo. That's a technical term, right?"

"Hell, you know what I mean." She didn't have to see him to know his jaw had just inched out a good mile or two. "Things start doing things they wouldn't otherwise when you use it. Right now we want all those things not doing anything. Nothing. Nada. No and triple nope. With 'not a chance in hell' thrown in for good measure. Do I make myself clear?"

"As mud."

"Good." He yawned. "It'll be dawn soon. We should try and catch some shut-eye."

"Works for me." She injected a note of enthusiasm into her words, while forgoing any hint of woo-woo. "And if any more of your buddies try and swipe your place in line, why you just saddle up and ride to the front of the pack on the first filly that comes to hand. That should beat 'em to the punch. How about it?"

He groaned. "I really wish you hadn't said that."

Good grief. "No saddling and riding, either? That must have been one strange dream."

"You have no idea." Then he completely baffled her by muttering, "Man, I hope your girl is a good runner. Though knowing you, she'll stand there and try and fight them off, one by one if necessary. Hell, I might as well face it. We're doomed."

She shook her head. Men. She didn't understand them when they were awake. She didn't have a hope in hades of understanding them when they were asleep. She shut her eyes.

"Good night, Lucien."

"Yeah, right. Maybe if all of us just settle down and go to sleep, we'll make it through this unscathed." He scooped her close again. "Good night, everybody."

Everybody? Raine's eyes popped open. Who the heck was everybody?

CHAPTER FIVE

A FAINT lightness invaded their cave, waking Lucien. He could sense the approach of others and glanced down at Raine, tucked close to his side. Soon it would begin— or end—depending on what happened next. He cautiously lifted his head, trying not to disturb her. The sheets were in a tangle at their feet, and off to one side he saw the scraps of feminine silk he'd stripped from her with such haste the night before.

The bra and panties were a heart-stopping, breath-snatching, all-lights-and-sirens-blaring, fire-engine red.

He grinned. Hell's bells. She'd ridden out to meet him wearing red silk beneath her work gear. It didn't matter whether she'd planned it beforehand. Fact was, she'd done it and he appreciated it more than he could say. He only wished he had time to explain the full extent of his appreciation. Unfortunately, there were more urgent topics to discuss in their few remaining moments together.

He studied her as he untangled a lock of raven-black hair that had become wound around his wrist. Even with dirt smudging her face and her hair caked with every manner of debris she was still beautiful. There was something noble about her, something painfully valiant. Few women he knew had endured the hardships she had and come out the other end stronger and more determined than before. He couldn't help but admire that particular quality.

Unable to resist, he bent toward her, waking her with

a kiss. Her lashes flickered against her cheeks and she opened her eyes. She stared at him silently, scanning his features as though committing them to memory. He regarded her just as intently. Her eyes were the most striking he'd ever seen, the gold-tinted green still awash with impossible dreams.

Her mouth trembled into a greeting. "Well, hey there," she murmured in a sleep-roughened voice. "You all recovered from your nightmares?"

He winced, images of yahooing men stampeding after a lone mare still playing in the back of his mind. "Might take a few weeks to make a full recovery." Not to mention a negative result on a certain pregnancy test.

Her brows drew together in concern. "Were they that bad?"

"Don't worry about it. It's not important."

He lowered his head to take her mouth again. Their lips clung, parted, and clung again. There was so much left unsaid. So much still to discuss. They needed to use these few remaining moments to talk, to reach some sort of agreement or understanding about how they intended to proceed from here. He started to suggest just that when a shout sounded from overhead.

"Hallooo! Anyone there?"

Lucien sat up. Closing his hand around Raine's undergarments, he tossed them to her. "Get dressed, sweetheart," he murmured. "Quiet, now."

Aside from a grimace of distaste, she didn't protest, but donned her bra and panties. "Aren't you going to let them know we're here?" she asked.

"In a sec."

As soon as she was dressed, he grabbed the sheets. He hated putting anything so dirty against her skin. Although when he compared it to the amount of dirt they'd accumulated during their adventures, he and Raine weren't much cleaner. And considering the alternative was walking out into the bright sunshine in their altogether, the sheets would have to do. He helped wrap one around her, before securing the other at his own waist.

Satisfied, he raised his voice. "Down here, Dobey," he called to his foreman.

"That you, boss?"

"Well, it sure as hell ain't Poke. Would you mind lending me a hand?"

"No sweat. We'll have you out of there in two shakes."

Lucien pulled Raine close and snatched a swift, hard kiss. "Get back out of sight. I'll chase my men off as quick as I can and then come for you."

"But—"

"Don't argue, Raine. You know how gossip travels around this place. No point in inviting trouble. Slide back under the roots of the tree and let's see if we can escape this with our skins—not to mention our reputations—intact."

She did as he ordered, but he could tell she didn't like it. A few minutes later, a hole opened above him and his foreman peered down. Catching sight of Lucien's getup, Dobey let out a shout of laughter.

"You boys ain't gonna believe this," he called over his shoulder.

"Don't just squat there gawking," Lucien grumbled. "Give me a hand up."

In no time they had him popped from his cavern and standing in the bright morning sunshine. It felt good to be fully upright with the sun warming his head and sufficient room to stretch his cramped limbs. Now if he could get rid of his men, Raine would be able to enjoy the same freedom.

"That's a mighty fine skirt you're wearing there, boss," Dobey observed. His thick white moustache capped a toothy grin. "Though not quite your usual style. Something happen to your britches?"

"Storm ate 'em."

"Must have been some storm."

"It was." Lucien turned to inspect the remains of the cabin, shocked into one of his more colorful expletives by what he saw. "That's all that's left?"

Dobey's amusement faded and he nodded grimly. "Gotta tell you, when we first rode up my heart sank straight down to my tippy toes. We didn't expect to find anyone alive under all that rubble. What didn't get gobbled up by the river got squashed flat by the tree."

He wasn't kidding. As far as Lucien could tell, not a single wall of the cabin remained. At some point, the section where he'd bedded down must have slid into the river along with the wood-burning stove. The only parts of the shack that hadn't vanished downstream were the sections of wall and roof that had become tangled in the branches of the tree. And even those were splintered into kindling. He'd had close calls before. But this... The muscles along his jaw bunched.

"We brung the horses," Dobey said.

Something in his foreman's tone snagged his attention and Lucien glanced past his men toward the string of horses they'd rode in on. Poke grazed nearby. And next to Poke stood Tickle. Hell. His foreman followed his gaze.

"The two wandered in together. Don't suppose you know the owner of the other horse?"

"Might."

"Well, if you don't, maybe she does." He inclined his head in the direction of the downed tree.

Raine had emerged from the hole while they'd stood there jawing. His men fell silent, staring. Not that he could blame them. She looked like an ancient goddess newly created from nature's bounty. Her hair captured the color of the night sky, and the twigs and leaves tangled within the hip-length tresses were reminiscent of the decoration gracing a noble headdress from a time long forgotten.

She stared calmly at the assembled riders, her eyes reflecting all the shades of a springtime forest, everything from the green of a newly unfurled leaf to that of a stately blue spruce. She stood as proud as mother nature, herself, her bare feet sunk deep into the earth from which she'd sprung, swaddled in a strip of ripped cloth that she wore with all the dignity and ease of a woman dressed for a coronation.

Her beauty was untamed and uncompromising and Lucien watched his men respond to it. The initial smirks faded, replaced by something akin to respect and awe. One by one, their gazes dropped before hers. All but the gaze of one of the newer hands, a tall, raw-boned kid who hadn't quite grown into his size.

The wrangler in question approached Lucien. "Something you should know," he murmured, his cold, black stare fixed on Raine.

"Spit it out, boy."

"Not where she can hear."

Lucien took instant exception to the way Rand said "she." He liked neither the tone, the look, nor the wrangler's stance. He deliberately knocked the kid back a pace, forcibly removing his gaze from where it didn't belong. "Speak your piece. Now."

"The fence to the south pasture's been cut. Deliberate. By the time we found out, her bull'd had himself a right good old time with that new breeding stock of Longhorns you brought in."

"When?"

"Sometime yesterday. Probably before the storm." His glance flickered in Raine's direction and then slid hastily away. "What do you want us to do about it?"

"Nothing. I'll deal with the fence." Lucien used a tone that should have put an end to the conversation.

Unfortunately, it didn't.

A smile cut a path beneath the shadow cast by the ranch hand's hat. "Wouldn't mind watchin' you deal with it, Kincaid."

Lucien turned on the kid, his anger flaring fast and hot. "That's Mr. Kincaid to you, boy. One more crack about matters that don't concern you and you can break out your bedroll and drift."

Outrage swept across the wrangler's expression. "You'd fire me? Over her?"

"Damn straight." He called to Dobey. "You and the boys move out. I'll meet up with you after I've found myself a working pair of britches."

Dobey took the hint. "You got it, boss. Shake a leg, boys. This old line shack won't be the only casualty from that storm. Let's find out what else we'll be busy fixing over the next week."

Rand hesitated and Lucien jerked his head toward the waiting horses. "You heard the foreman. Get going. And think on what I said, boy. Think on it long and hard."

"Yessir, Mr. Kincaid. I'll be sure to do that."

Lucien watched as his men rode off. There was a brief discussion between them before Dobey called a sharp halt to it. Lucien had a fair notion who was the main topic of that discussion and which of his men had precipitated the dialogue. The next time he found Dobey alone, he'd ask his foreman to keep an eye on the new fellow. He had a sneaking suspicion that Rand wouldn't last much longer. Something about the kid felt wrong and he'd learned long ago to trust his instincts when it came to the three most important things in life—people, animals, and poker.

He started to tug his Stetson lower on his brow, before recalling that he'd lost it along with his clothes when the line shack had collapsed. Hell. It was his favorite one, too.

"Rosie just got in a fresh supply of hats yesterday," Raine offered. "She even has the style you prefer. Won't take much to beat it into shape. Just lose your temper a time or two and it'll be battered good and proper."

He grinned. Okay, so he had a tendency to throw down his hat when he got peeved. He wasn't the only one. He'd seen Raine bury her Stetson in the dirt a time or two. "With you around, I don't doubt it."

Her amusement matched his. "We do seem to have that affect on each other."

She approached and Lucien had trouble tearing his gaze from her. Where he looked ridiculous in his sheet, she looked magnificent. He'd just have preferred she not share all that magnificence with his wranglers.

He cleared his throat. "So, why did you come out from under that tree? I thought I told you to stay put."

"You may have told me, but that doesn't mean I have to listen." She shrugged. "Besides, there wasn't any point in hiding once I realized your men had Tickle with them."

His curiosity got the better of him. "You knew she was here? How?"

"Hard to explain." She wrinkled her brow in thought. "The best way I can describe it is that I sensed her."

Some men might laugh off the possibility, but Lucien had seen Raine's gift in action too many times to discount it. "Well, you sensed right. I suppose there wasn't any point in hiding after that."

It didn't matter, he decided. They'd just brazen their way through any talk that resulted. And the first man who said something untoward would find his face on the wrong side of Lucien's fist, just like last time. He flexed his hands in preparation, wincing as his wrist voiced an objection to the proposed activity. He deliberately ignored the pain. He liked it when his problems had such simplistic solutions, and this was as simple as they came, despite his wrist. One swift punch would take care of the least important of the two issues he faced.

Now to see if the other matter was as easy to resolve. He glanced at Raine and grimaced. Knowing her tendency for bullheadedness, he doubted anything about the next few minutes would prove easy. Not that it mattered. One way or another they'd come to an agreement. The only question was whether they'd come to it without locking horns…or like two headstrong bulls fighting over ownership of one tiny pen.

"This strikes me as a good time to decide where we go from here," he offered as an opening gambit.

"What do you mean?"

Okay, fine. If she wanted to paw at the ground and bellow a challenge, he'd be happy to do some pawing and bellowing of his own. "In case you missed it, sweetheart, our relationship changed last night."

An infuriating remoteness clung to her. "Because we had sex?"

"We didn't have sex, dammit!" Too bad he hadn't

already bought his new hat. This would have provided an excellent opportunity to throw it into the dirt. Maybe even stomp on it a few times. Give it a kick or two. "You have to know the difference between an evening of 'howdy ma'am, hope you don't mind if I keep my boots on,' and what happened between us last night."

The remoteness fell away and she chuckled. "'Hope you don't mind if I keep my boots on'? Is that how you typically do it, Kincaid?"

"Depends on the woman," he muttered. He allowed his irritation to show. "Let me guess. Your lovers take off their boots."

"And their hats, too."

"I'm surprised Nanna hasn't had words about that."

"She did the last time it happened. And I expect she will this time, too," Raine replied calmly.

It took a full minute for comprehension to set in. "You've only...? Just twice?" He couldn't believe it. "You mean, you and me? That's it?"

She shook her head in admiration. "Hot damn, Kincaid. No grass grows under your feet, does it?"

A fierce possessiveness threatened his self-control. "How the hell was I supposed to know? You're thirty years old, for crying out loud. I'd have thought—" He stopped talking before he dug himself in any deeper.

Raine folded her arms across her chest. It was such a defensive gesture that it was all he could do not to gather her up in his arms. Unfortunately, he didn't think she'd appreciate the gesture. Not in her current mood. He kept his mouth shut, giving her a chance to regain her poise.

She faced him with a touching bravado. "You might recall I lost my grandfather right after our last visit to the line shack. I was an eighteen-year-old kid with no parents, no grandfather, a ranch to run, and a grandmother to take care of. That didn't leave me a lot of time for…'' She lifted her shoulders and a hint of red flashed from beneath the sheet. ''Visiting line shacks.''

He cleared his throat. ''Well, if you had visited a few more, you'd have a basis for comparison. Not that I'm suggesting such a thing—''

''No, of course not,'' she retorted dryly.

He plowed on, fully aware he was making a complete ass of himself, but unable to help it. ''If you'd been with…with—''

''Others?''

''Yeah, others.'' Great gobs of cow hockey! Where was the exit door to this conversation? ''If you'd been with others, you'd know that our situation was unique.''

''I'll keep that in mind. I'll also remember to insist on no hats and boots.''

He released his breath in a gusty sigh. ''Hell. You're making fun of me, aren't you?''

She finally relented. ''Just a little.''

Somehow he suspected this conversation would be going better if he had A: more sleep, B: a gallon of thick-as-tar coffee zinging through his veins, C: something other than a sheet wrapped around his middle, and D: fewer hormones. In fact ''D'' alone was driving him insane. The best he could tell, every last hormone he possessed found Raine's sheet-wrapped status of supreme temptation. He shook his head in an effort to bring even one sleep-deprived brain cell on line.

''Let me get this straight,'' he said. ''We're supposed to forget about last night? Pretend it never happened?''

''Yes.''

He'd suspected that would be her decision. Having it confirmed aggravated him beyond measure. ''You're going to treat this like last time, aren't you?'' Her silence was all the answer he needed. "Dammit, woman! I know you had it rough all those years ago. What happened with Paps was a horrible accident. I tried to help afterward. I swear, I did my level best. But in those weeks before Nanna hustled you off to college, you wouldn't let me anywhere near the ranch. As I recall, the last time I showed up, you pulled a shotgun on me. Hell, you blasted the tips of my boots clean off. And they were my best boots, too."

Her chin climbed a notch. "Paps meant everything to me. Accident or no, you took him from me over a foolish land dispute. A relationship with you was out of the question. Since you had trouble understanding that simple fact, I thought the shotgun would clarify the matter."

"Oh, it clarified the matter just fine. Next time you try and clarify matters like that, expect me to take serious objection." He let the gravity of his objection rumble through his voice. "Nobody points the wrong end of a shotgun in my direction and gets away with it more than once. It's dangerous. And after what happened to Paps, I'd have thought you'd realize just how dangerous."

A hint of color bloomed across her cheekbones. Temper, no doubt. It sure as hell couldn't be embarrassment. Not from Ms. Attitude. "If it makes you feel any better, Nanna practically skinned me alive. She even dragged me into Sheriff Tilson's office so he could chew me out for a spell."

A slow smile built across his mouth. "I always did have a soft spot for Nanna."

She continued with dogged determination. "Shotguns aside, there were other factors that kept me from trusting you."

Uh-oh. "Such as?"

"You talk too much, Kincaid. No one needed to know that we had sex. But you saw to it that they did."

"First, stop calling it sex. You're doing it deliberately to rile me."

"Is it working?"

"I'd think the steam pouring out of my ears would be answer enough." She took the hint and didn't push further. "And second, that's twice in the last twenty-four hours that you've accused me of running my mouth about that first night we made love. It's past time I set the record straight. I didn't then, nor have I since, told anyone what happened between us. Not ever. Got it?"

"People found out somehow. I didn't tell them. That only leaves you."

There was one unfortunate flaw to her logic. A few other people had known the truth. His grandparents…and hers. But he couldn't tell her that without revealing the rest of it. And he had no intention of adding to her hurt.

"I'll say this one last time," he gritted out. "I didn't tell a living soul what happened between us that night."

"Then how did they find out?"

He buttoned his lip, knowing full well that it damned him.

She nodded, the brightness fading from her eyes, leaving them flat and dark. "That's what I thought." She turned toward Tickle. "I only have one last question before I go."

"Shoot," he said, then added wryly, "Figuratively speaking, of course."

"What did that kid say to you?"

"What kid?"

She glanced over her shoulder. "Don't play games,

Kincaid. That new wrangler. Rand. He told you some-thing. Something you didn't like.''

So they were back to last names. Figured. Why should today be different from any other? No doubt she was busy forging as many fences as possible to separate them. The minute one fence fell, another got thrown up to replace it. ''Seems we've had a small accident.''

Alarm skittered across her face. ''Nanna?''

How did she do it? Here he'd done the polite thing and hauled his backside onto his half of the property line and with one simple look, she had him leaping barbed wire to get to her. ''Nothing like that,'' he reassured. ''Best as anyone knows, Nanna's fine.''

Relief etched lines of weariness across her dirt-smudged face. ''Then what's wrong?''

He hesitated. This was one of those discussions which might be better accomplished after he'd taken care of ''A'' through ''D'' on his list. Particularly ''B.'' Man, he'd kill for some coffee right about now. Raine shifted from one foot to the other, prompting a reply. ''My fence's been cut,'' he told her.

That garnered her full attention. She regarded him warily. ''Which one?''

''The south pasture.''

She smiled without amusement. ''The Disputed Land.''

He rose to the bait like a trout to the perfect lure. ''It's not in dispute anymore, if you'll recall. It's Kincaid land now and your bull got at those new longhorns I brought in last month.''

''You're sure it's been cut?'' she asked skeptically. ''It didn't come down in the storm?''

Either she didn't know anything about it or she was a damned good liar. ''Tell me something, Featherstone.

Just out of curiosity, why did you move your bull to that particular pasture?''

Anger rippled across her expression and she drew herself up in an aggressive stance. ''You making an accusation or just running your mouth?''

''You didn't put him there until after I moved those longhorns in.''

''So?''

''So somebody's set my breeding program back on its heels and I'm trying to figure out who.''

''You think it's deliberate.''

''Once I take a look at that fence, I'll know for sure. But, yeah. I think it's deliberate.''

''For your information, that piece of property you took from Nanna connects two of our pastures and I used to drive my cattle through there on a regular basis.'' A hint of disillusionment darkened her eyes. ''Now that you've turned it into a dead end, I put Old Bullet there to keep him out of harm's way. Since he can barely move from one end of the pasture to the other, I seriously doubt he could have find the wherewithal to impregnate your cows. Satisfied?''

No, he wasn't the least satisfied. He wouldn't be until he'd broken down every last fence she'd put between them. Wisely, he kept that comment to himself. ''Fair enough,'' he replied.

She turned on her heel and crossed to where Tickle stood patiently waiting. Without the least sign of self-consciousness, she hitched up her sheet, exposing an endless length of smooth, shapely leg. Then, grasping the saddlehorn, she vaulted straight onto her horse's back in a move he'd watched her master in her teens. She sat tall and straight, gathering the reins in one hand. The blood of her ancestors had never been more obvious. A haughty pride rode her face, accented by the tilt of her chin and the coolness in her eyes. It took every ounce of control not to tip her out of that saddle and carry her back to their earthen cave in order to take up where they'd last left off.

"I didn't cut your fence," she repeated. "But that won't last much longer. As soon as I find Nanna's letter, I'm reclaiming our land. And when I do, I plan to rip that fence down post by post."

She didn't wait for his response. A single word murmured beneath her breath had Tickle exploding into motion. Horse and rider took the rise at a dead run, Raine's hair snapping behind her in a long flag of feminine defiance. Of even greater interest was her sheet. It unraveled with each pounding hoof beat, winking and waving a sassy farewell. He didn't move a muscle until she disappeared from sight.

With a sigh of regret, he leaned against his horse. "That went well, don't you think?" Poke swung his head around and butted Lucien's shoulder, knocking him back on his heels. No question whose side his horse had taken. "Hey, it could be worse. She could have ridden off with you in tow and made me hike home in this blasted sheet."

Poke released a snort that sounded suspiciously like amusement.

Lucien turned on the horse, outraged. "Why, you old son of a gun. She wouldn't have needed to tow you along behind. If she'd have called, you'd have gone, wouldn't you have?"

Poke didn't need to answer.

His smug grin said it all.

CHAPTER SIX

"SHE'LL be down any minute." Nanna crossed to the stove in easy strides identical to her granddaughter's and stirred a huge vat of some unidentifiable concoction that looked disgusting, but smelled incredible. The pervasive scent of cinnamon filled the air creating the overall impression of hearth and home. "She rode in an hour ago and went straight from the barn to the bathroom. Hasn't been out since."

"I'm sorry, Nanna," Shadoe said. "I didn't mean to put them at risk. If I'd realized a storm was brewing—"

"All that storm did was bring about the inevitable." She turned and glanced at Shadoe, offering a quick, warm smile. "You may be interested to know she wasn't wearing any clothes when she slipped in. Leastwise, none to speak of."

Shadoe's brows shot up. "Interesting development. What do you suppose happened?"

"Only thing that can happen when a man and a woman return home buck naked."

He grinned. "I meant to their clothes."

A distant look dimmed her pale green eyes. "Storm ate 'em," she murmured.

"Wow. Must have been one heck of a storm."

"That it was."

He leaned across the table, his expression one of regret. "You realize this is as far as the Cupid Committee can interfere?"

Nanna inclined her head. "I remember all your ifs,

96

buts, and wherefores. Don't expect we'll need any further help. Fate's taken over from where you left off.''

"Great. Then my job is done.''

"And what job is that?'' Raine appeared in the doorway, her braided hair still damp from her shower. At her heels stood a black-and-white border collie who managed to look both oddly concerned and highly indignant, the two reactions in clear defense of his mistress. "Or should I guess what you've been up to? And once I'm done guessing, how 'bout I knock you on your backside, you lousy son of a—''

"Raine!'' her grandmother cut in. "Mind your tongue.''

Shadoe climbed to his feet. "Hello, to you, too. Good seeing you again.''

Raine stepped into the room, her collie, Dog, glued to her side. "Give it to me straight, Shadoe. Were you behind what happened last night? Yes or no.'' After a quick glance at his mistress, Dog underscored the question with a low growl.

"Some of it, yes,'' Shadoe admitted.

She'd suspected as much the minute she'd found him making himself at home at her grandmother's kitchen table. She'd learned at Emma's wedding that Shadoe was the Cupid Committee's main Instigator. If he was here, there could only be one explanation. Even so, she found the confirmation upsetting. "You sent a note to Lucien and signed my name to it?''

"Guilty.''

"And you sent another in his handwriting to me?''

"Yes.''

"You mind telling me what the hell you were thinking?'' She paced from one end of the sizable room to the other. Dog bounced alongside, his doggy pleasure in the fruitless exercise at direct odds to her irritability. Every once in a while, he broke stride long enough to look upward, as though attempting to judge whether he was doing his job right. Satisfied, he resumed his bouncing step with renewed enthusiasm. "You could have gotten us killed, Shadoe."

"I'm truly sorry about that. I didn't realize there was a storm moving in or I would have waited another day to send those notes."

She swivelled to face him, nearly colliding with the collie. "Good grief. Take point, Dog, before I run you down." Instantly, the collie went nose to kneecap with Shadoe and offered a doggy grin filled with sharp, white teeth. "Then you weren't trying to trap us at the cabin?"

Shadoe hesitated, inching away from the collie. Not that it helped. Dog inched right along with him, teeth first. "Trap, no. I was giving you an opportunity to take advantage of a private getaway if you felt so inclined."

"Lucien and I despise each other." Dog's hungry grin vanished and he swivelled to stare at her in such comical surprise that hot color suffused her cheeks. Darn animal. She shouldn't have told him about last night. He never could keep his thoughts to himself, no matter how many times she warned him. What with Nanna and Shadoe watching, her only option was to brazen it out and hope they didn't catch on. "Why would you think Lucien and I'd feel inclined to do anything other than throw a few punches?"

Shadoe glanced from Dog to her and lifted an eyebrow. "Is that what you two did all night? Punch each other?"

More hot color poured into her cheeks. "We managed to restrain ourselves," she lied without compunction. She pretended not to hear Dog's snicker. Definitely time to reset a few boundaries with the rotten mutt. He'd gotten far too free with his opinion of late, a fact she'd explain to him in no uncertain terms. "But it wasn't easy."

Nanna turned from the stove. "I'm relieved to hear it." No question whether she'd picked up on Dog's reaction. She didn't even bother to hide her amusement. "I'd have had to reassess my opinion of Lucien if all you'd done is fight."

"Why do I have the feeling you have something to do with this mess?" Raine asked.

"Because I do."

"You approached the Cupid Committee?"

"I did."

"But why?"

Nanna smiled sadly. "You know why. You can't manage on your own. With the financial setbacks we've had these past few years, you've had to let go of half our wranglers. Once upon a time, I could have picked up the slack. But I can't anymore. Soon I won't be of any help at all."

Raine was by her side in an instant. "Don't you ever say that," she ordered fiercely, wrapping her arms around her grandmother. Dog joined the family circle, nudging between them and offering supportive licks. "You'll always be a help to me."

Nanna shook her head. "You need more than I can offer. Our predicament is only going to get worse with time and I worry about your future." She cupped Raine's face. "Look at these past months. Your two best friends got married and you were forced to cut your visits short because you couldn't afford the time away from here. You spend your life working this ranch instead of living life on a ranch. There's a difference, you know. I want you happy with a man of your own and a family. I want to see you settled.''

"You're my family," Raine argued fiercely. "I don't need anyone else. You, of all people, should know that a man doesn't guarantee happiness. We create our own.''

Nanna patted Raine's cheek. "I'm not disputing that, sweetheart. You've carved out a wonderful life for yourself. But it's not complete. Do you think I can't sense that you want more?''

The comment kicked Raine into motion again and she untangled herself from Nanna's embrace before swallowing the length of the room in a few jerky steps. If only it was as easy to distance herself from the discussion. "You believe Lucien's the more I want?" she asked once she'd ran out of maneuvering space. She glanced over her shoulder at her grandmother. "And what if he is? How can you forgive him after what he did to Paps? How can you welcome him into our family?''

"It was an accident, Raine. A horrible tragedy, one Lucien would do anything to change.'' Tears glistened in Nanna's eyes. "Has it ever occurred to you that the outcome that day might have been different? What if the situation had been reversed and Lucien had been the one to die, would you have forgiven Paps?''

It didn't take any thought. "Of course." Raine closed her eyes, the logic of Nanna's argument hitting home. "Of course, I'd forgive Paps.''

"It's time to let Lucien off the hook, pigeon. It's time to get on with your life. I've noticed you taking the measure of some of the unattached men in town, wondering if they stand as tall as Lucien. None of them do. None of them could.''

"You think Lucien is my private measuring stick?" she asked.

Nanna's smile lit up her face, vanquishing her tears. "You've had a hankering for that Kincaid boy since the first time you set eyes on him. And he hasn't been able to keep his hands off you since you were both old enough to know what the opposite in opposite sex actually meant."

Raine shook her head. "A hankering isn't enough for marriage." She addressed Shadoe. "I assume that's where you were hoping this was headed? Marriage?"

"That's our goal," he agreed.

"Sorry to disappoint you, but it's not going to happen."

"Oh, I wouldn't count us out just yet."

Anger battled with an overwhelming urge to burst into tears. It had to be from exhaustion. A sleepless night had made her vulnerable. There was no other reasonable explanation. Otherwise she wouldn't find the suggestion of marriage so incredibly appealing. She fought to regain control, to stand strong against both Shadoe and her grandmother.

"You two aren't listening. Lucien Kincaid and I aren't getting married. No way, no how. He's nothing but six foot four inches of pure, unadulterated thieving nastiness. You really want to saddle me with someone like that?" she asked Shadoe.

He shook his head. "I have to admit, when you put it like that, it does make me hesitate."

"And well it should." She switched her attention to Nanna. "What about you? Are you still intent on playing matchmaker?"

"You're going to marry him, pigeon. It's inevitable." Raine wasn't the only one with a gift. Her grandmother possessed one, as well. Where Raine had a talent with animals, Nanna's was more of a "knowing." No one dared argue when she voiced one of her opinions, particularly not when stated with such authority.

"He doesn't want to marry me," Raine argued. "If it happens, what sort of marriage will we end up with? Not one I'd care to contemplate."

"It will work."

"Then why involve the Cupid Committee? If it was going to happen, why couldn't it occur naturally?"

"Because you and Lucien are too stubborn. You've turned away from every opportunity." Nanna folded her arms across her chest. Between her height, the light of battle in her eyes, and the resoluteness of her expression, it was a formidable stance. "It was time to create an opportunity you couldn't turn from."

"Great. What happened to free will?"

Nanna didn't back down an inch. "You've been free to be as willful as you've wanted for the past thirty years. Now you pay the price for it."

"Has anyone taken into consideration how Lucien will feel about this? I don't think he'll take kindly to having his future manipulated, any more than I do."

"That depends on what that future holds for him. You have a say in that. You can choose to make it heaven. Or you can make it a living hell."

Raine fixed her gaze on the gleaming linoleum at her feet as she considered her grandmother's words. Last night had been heaven, no question. But with the first light of day that had changed. Didn't Nanna understand? She and Lucien weren't meant to be together. They were opposites, from their personalities to their preferences, right down to the Disputed Land, they sat on opposite sides of an impenetrable fence. What did it matter that the two times they'd come together had been the most amazing of her life? Opposites could occasionally make an interesting whole. But more often they simply remained in opposition.

Lucien Kincaid was a taker. Even if she forgave him for Paps, he'd still taken her innocence, her reputation, and her land. The only thing he hadn't taken—at least recently—was her heart and she planned to keep it that way. A violent force of nature had brought them together. But it had only needed a casual word from one of Lucien's wranglers to drive them apart again. What chance did marriage stand against that?

None.

Raine regarded her grandmother once again, a grim determination giving steely emphasis to her stance. "You've made a mistake, Nanna. Marriage to Lucien is out of the questions. You shouldn't have interfered." She glanced at Shadoe, jerking her thumb toward the door. "As for you, by the time I get back, I expect you to have cleared out. Fair warning, Cupid Man. You and that committee of yours are to stay away from me and my grandmother or there'll be hell to pay."

Raine ate up the distance between house and barn in swift, angry strides. Saddling Tickle, she whistled for Dog and rode out in the direction of what remained of her north pasture—at least, the part Lucien hadn't annexed. She wanted to take a look at that fence line and check on Old Bullet. She also wanted some quiet time to cool off and put the events of the past twenty-four hours into perspective.

Having both horse and dog with her helped. There was something soothing about animals. Their needs and emotions were basic, and therefore understandable. Even cats made sense to her, no doubt because their sheer contrariness often matched her own. Push them in one direction and they took the other, leaving behind a few scratches as a testament to feline superiority in the face of human idiocy. A perfectly normal reaction, as far as Raine was concerned. Whereas a dog would suffer any manner of indignity for a kind word, cats were intent on their own comfort, no matter the inconvenience to mankind or fellow creature. She'd always admired that sort of brazenness.

Topping a ridge, she looked down toward the stretch of land that marked the northern border of her property and the southern end of Kincaid land. A healthy river divided the two sections, a river that had once been her exclusive property. Not anymore. Ever since Lucien had staked his claim, posts had been set, barbed wire had been strung and she'd been forced to drill for the water her cattle had once enjoyed in abundance.

Clicking her tongue, she urged Tickle toward the fence line. Rounding a honey mesquite tree, she peered underneath. Old Bullet enjoyed both the shade, as well as rubbing against the trunk of the huge, old tree. He was also known to snap up any mesquite beans that came his way. Unfortunately, the bull was nowhere to be seen. She whistled an off-tune song, one that usually brought the old boy running. This time, silence greeted her call and she made a silent note to send one of her men out after him to check on his condition. If he had broken through the fence onto Kincaid land, she was fairly certain Lucien's hands hadn't been particularly gentle when they'd returned him.

Circling the tree, she discovered Lucien crouched on his side of the property line, examining the fence in question. He looked up at her approach, tipping his

Stetson to the back of his head. It was his Sunday best, as were his boots, and told her something about his list of priorities. Obviously checking the fence ranked right at the top. With an excited bark, Dog deserted her in favor of male companionship. Streaking beneath the fence, he lavished Lucien with an unwarranted amount of affection. Lucien took the tongue-washing in stride while Raine viewed the animal's turncoat behavior with grumpy disgust.

"Well?" she called to Lucien. The word came out more clipped than she liked and she fought to moderate it. It wasn't his fault that her dog was such a poor judge of character. "Did Old Bullet force a hole through your fence or was it cut?"

"Both. Looks like the fence sustained a bit of damage before it was cut."

Odd. "How did that happen?"

"I'm not sure, but I mean to find out."

He appeared far too grim for her peace of mind and she switched her attention to his cattle. They milled in the distance at the river's edge of what was once Featherstone property. "And your longhorns?"

"My problem. I'll deal with it."

Raine had to hand it to him. Lucien had a knack for politely slamming the door on a discussion. She'd never acquired the talent, herself, but it was impressive to watch. Unfortunately, it didn't leave her much in the way of a conversational follow-up. What was she supposed to say? "Gee, nice night we had. We'll have to do it again sometime." Right. That would go over well.

She eyed Lucien. Maybe too well. Maybe so well that he'd pluck her out of the saddle and turn "sometime" into right here and now. Her thighs tightened around Tickle and she yanked her hat so low on her forehead she could barely see out from beneath the brim. Time was wasting and she had a lot of property to check for storm damage.

She broached the only topic available to her. It was also the one she least wanted to address. "There's something you should know," she announced with notable reluctance.

"Let me guess. You found out who sent the notes."

"Yes." She found the admission harder than she'd thought possible. "Nanna called in the Cupid Committee."

"Nanna." His expression eased and he shook his head, a smile touching the corners of his mouth. "Meddling old woman."

"You don't look terribly upset." Her brows pulled together. "Or surprised."

"She's the only one I could think of who'd pull such a fool stunt."

"You calling my grandmother a fool?"

He stilled, the gaze he trained on her sharpening. "I'm calling her actions foolish," he stated evenly. "There's a difference."

"A mighty fine one."

He slowly rose. Spreading two lines of barbed wire, he stepped through. One of the points snagged his shirt, nicking both the heavy cotton and the skin beneath. But then, that's what happened when you crossed lines that shouldn't be crossed. Reaching up, he helped her off Tickle. It didn't matter that she wasn't interested in leaving the safety of her horse. Lucien never worried about such minor details as those. Dog continued with his traitorous ways and didn't put up so much as a token protest. Instead, he wagged his tail and offered a knowing grin.

"That's better," Lucien said. "Now why don't you yank that burr out from under your saddlebags and tell me what's got you all worked up?"

"I don't like having my life manipulated."

"In case you've forgotten, I'm not the one pulling the strings. In fact, my strings have been tugged right alongside of yours."

True enough, though that didn't change anything. She preferred making her own decisions in life, not having them foisted on her. Of course, Lucien was the same way, maybe even more so. Right from the get-go, he'd been determined to forge his own path through life. She'd always admired that about him. And because it was a character trait so similar to her own, he deserved both her respect and as calm and reasonable a discussion of their problems as possible.

"Give me an honest answer, Kincaid. And don't add any ribbons and bows to pretty it up. Do you think I cut your fence?"

"No. Is that plain enough for you?"

She blinked in surprise. "Why not?"

"Because you're not a vindictive woman. Ornery, yeah. But not vindictive." He frowned at the stretch of fence in question and hunkered down to study it again. Dog gave him another cheerful lick and then trotted off, pursuing various doggy pastimes that involved a lot of sniffing and snuffling and grass rolling. "Looks to me like this section has been repaired more than once. I'm guessing Old Bullet knocked against it on a regular basis trying to bust through. He must have made life pretty miserable for the wrangler assigned to repair it."

She nodded, crouching beside him. "Old Bullet was mighty fond of water. Makes sense he'd try and get to it, especially if it meant frolicking with some friendly neighboring cows." Her brows drew together. "But why would one of your own wranglers cut the fence? That doesn't add up."

"It does if he left the job half done because bad weather was moving in, or he didn't have the supplies he needed for the repair, or it was chow time and he was too impatient to finish the job first. Maybe your bull wasn't on this side of the pasture and the kid thought he'd have time to get the repairs done later in the day."

It took her a minute to understand where Lucien was headed. "And Old Bullet took advantage of such fool-hardy thinking and ambled on through to enjoy a visit with your cows."

"When the wrangler returned and saw what had happened, he decided to cut the wire so it looked like someone from your side of the fence had done it on purpose to ruin my breeding stock. That way he could shift the blame and wouldn't lose his job over an act of sheer stupidity."

Raine rocked back on her heels and shoved her Stetson to the back of her head. "Interesting theory, but how do you prove it?"

"My problem. I'll deal with it."

She released her breath in an exasperated sigh. "In case no one's bothered to tell you, you're real irritating when you slam the door on a conversation like that."

He turned his head to look at her, his gaze uncomfortably intent. His eyes were midnight-dark and filled with an emotion she didn't dare name. Memories of the previous night lingered there, reminding her of the intimacy they'd shared—an intimacy she'd just as soon forget. The blackness of night coupled with the gravity of their predicament had allowed her to take chances she never would have under normal circumstances. It had also allowed her to respond without the restraints imposed by age or wisdom or basic common sense. She'd been too busy feeling instead of thinking, always a bad choice.

She shot to her feet and put some maneuvering space between them. "So what now?"

"In case you hadn't noticed, you're not half bad at door slamming, yourself."

"Another example of why a relationship between us would never work out," she replied. "All that slamming would bring the house down around our ears."

A grin appeared beneath the shadow of his hat. "Been there, done that. Just last night, in case you've forgotten. Personally, I thought bringing down the house worked rather well for us."

Before she could respond to the gibe, Dog came streaking across the grass, barking wildly. Even if she hadn't been attuned to the animals in her care, she'd have known something was wrong. "Show me, Dog," she ordered.

Before she could take more than a step, Lucien settled a heavy hand on her shoulder, stopping her in her tracks. "Don't go."

"I have to." She reached down and quieted Dog with a gentle touch. "Something's wrong."

"I know. I was about to tell you about it."

She turned and stared at him with gut-wrenching apprehension. "What is it?"

"I don't know how to break this to you, other than to tell you straight. I'm sorry, honey. Old Bullet's been shot."

She didn't hesitate, but started in the direction Dog had come from. She only managed two steps before Lucien overtook her. He circled in front of her, blocking her path. "Move, Kincaid," she ordered. Pain ripped through her voice, causing the words to grate. "I have an animal to see to."

"There's nothing you can do. Trust me. You don't want to see this, Raine. Let me take care of it."

"Why?" Her hands closed into fists. She stared over his shoulder toward a mound of darkness shielded by scrub, and tears burned in her eyes. "You think your man is responsible?"

He drew her back toward Tickle and the battered fence line. "I intend to find out. If he is, I'll replace the animal."

She spared one final glance backward, wiping at her eyes with the cuff of her sleeve. "And you'll fire the one who did it?"

"You have my word. I don't abide this sort of behavior. You know that."

"I don't know much of anything anymore. At one time I wouldn't have thought you a claim jumper. But here I sit staring at a fence that cuts me off from what should be Featherstone property."

"Don't go there, Raine." Exhaustion dogged him. "There's no point."

She didn't argue further. He couldn't decide if that was good, or a problem in the making. There were times when he found her impossible to read. She swept all of her passion behind an impenetrable mask where he couldn't see or sense or touch her thoughts. He knew she was hurting, but he didn't know how to ease that hurt, not as long as she kept herself closed off from him.

There was one final subject he wanted to broach before they parted. "We have some decisions to make."

She folded her arms around her waist and took another step backward. "What decisions?"

Raine hadn't always been this defensive and regret filled him. He remembered a time when every emotion had blazed across her face and fairy tales had glittered like pixie dust in her eyes. She'd been joyous and romantic and filled with a belief in making dreams come true. It was his fault those dreams had died.

He'd taken her joy and romantic nature and instead of giving her the dreams she craved, he'd killed them. Because of one foolish error in judgment, an instinctive reaction that he'd spent a dozen years regretting, her life had taken a path she'd never intended. His mouth tightened. He'd failed to protect her then. He wouldn't fail her again. Once this business with Old Bullet was sorted out, he'd give her the fairy tale. He'd make her believe again.

"Decisions," she prompted. "You said we had decisions to make."

"Right. Let's start with this one." Unable to resist, he pulled her close and settled his mouth on hers.

She hesitated for a timeless moment. And then she swayed against him, lifting to him. He wrapped his arms around her, absorbing the unmistakable impact of a femininity as strong as it was soft. All thoughts of fences or property disputes or the bittersweet history they shared faded from existence. They were simply a man and a woman embracing beneath a sun-filled blue sky, doing what came natural to them. And right now "natural" meant an urgent tangle of arms and legs and tongues.

He cupped her bottom, lifting her closer and her hat tumbled to the ground. She shifted her hips to accommodate him, straining for a closeness impeded by thick, sturdy denim. If her groan of frustration was anything to go by, she found the barriers thwarting them as infuriating as he did. He wanted to strip away her clothes, to lower her to the ground and take her with the same possessive urgency they'd shared the night before.

He fumbled with his gloves, ripping them from his hands and tossing them aside. Then he yanked her shirt free of her waistband and tore the snaps apart. She smelled like heaven. If hunger were a perfume, it would belong exclusively to Raine. The crisp odor of soap combined with an earthy muskiness that threatened his sanity. He remembered that scent, reveled in it. It belonged to the darkest of stormy nights, to rich, damp earth and desperate lovemaking. It belonged to a pleasure so intense it defied comprehension. For one short night they'd been stripped of civilized behavior, leaving them at their most primitive—and most painfully honest.

"I want you." He fitted his hands to her silk-covered breasts and took her mouth in long, lingering kisses. "It's only been a few hours and yet, if I don't have you again, I think I'll go mad."

"We can't." Her hold on him tightened, giving lie to her words. "You know we can't."

"There's nothing stopping us," he argued. "We're grown adults, Raine. We don't need anyone's permission to make love."

"Stop using that word." She gasped for air. "It's not love."

Her denial infuriated him. "How can you be so sure? We've felt this way for years."

"We felt this way once. When we were young and foolish. It's just been a while, is all. We're both feeling…itchy."

"We scratched that itch last night. It hasn't gone away. If anything, it's gotten worse."

"Then put some calamine lotion on it," she ordered fiercely. "Bathe in oatmeal."

He chuckled. "Is that what you plan to do?"

"If that's what it takes, then yes. Hell, Kincaid, I'd let my ranch hands strip me naked and dip me in a vat full of bug killer if it meant getting you out from under my skin."

He buried his amusement behind a quick kiss. She fought so hard against the inevitable. But she wasn't going to win. He couldn't let her destroy what they felt before it had a chance to grow into what it was meant to become. When he came up for air, he cupped her face, forcing her to look at him. "You've got it all wrong, sweetheart. What we're feeling isn't a bug or even a rash."

"Then what is it?"

"Wildflowers. They crop up where they shouldn't, bringing life and color to barren earth. We tried weeding them out once before. We almost succeeded. But when we weren't looking, they spread far and wide until now there are too many to pull."

"Flowers?" She shivered. "Flowers are making me feel this way?"

"Lots and lots of flowers. Give in, Raine. Give in to what you want."

He slid his thumbs across the peaked tips of her breasts and she sank against him. Sunlight blazed downward revealing all that the darkness had kept from him when he'd last held her. Passion gave her an incandescent beauty, turning her eyes the most incredible shade of green he'd ever seen. A desperate want gleamed there, emotions that spoke only to him, that burned for him alone. All that she'd fought to keep hidden was bared for him to see, a truth so deep and unwavering that he didn't dare believe it.

"Let go, sweetheart. Tell me what you're feeling."

He'd pushed too soon and too hard. Instantly the shutters slammed down. "No." She tore free of his arms. "No. I won't go through this again. Once was bad enough."

He regarded her warily. "Go through what again?"

"Loving you."

The unguarded admission shocked him, even as it filled him with a surge of fierce pleasure. "You at risk for that?" She made a move toward Tickle and he caught hold of her arm, spinning her around before she could make good her escape. "Answer me, Raine," he demanded urgently. "Are you still at risk?"

"What the hell do you think, Kincaid?" She fumbled with her shirt, shoving it into her waistband and closing as many snaps as her shaking fingers could manage. "I loved you when I was eighteen and look what happened."

"Raine—"

She shook him off. "No! Not again. I lost everything last time I allowed myself to fall in love. My grandfather. My reputation. My future." Her eyes burned with a harsh iridescence. "You."

"You didn't lose me. You left me. It was your choice."

"I didn't have any other choice. Not after Paps died. That one night at the line shack started a chain of events we couldn't escape. Not then and not now. I'm not about to allow last night to start another."

Whether she realized it or not, a new chain of events had already been put into motion. And it couldn't be stopped this time, any more than last. "Give it a chance, honey. That's all I'm asking. We can start over and see where it leads."

"Can we?" The light died from her eyes. "Can you

bring back Old Bullet? Can you restore my reputation this time around? And what about my land? Will you give it back to me? Is that how you plan to start over?''

He shook his head, knowing it would condemn him. Old Bullet was dead and there was no bringing him back. As for the land, he couldn't return it to her anymore than he could explain why. Hell, he couldn't even salvage her reputation. People would talk no matter how many heads he busted. In fact, busting heads would only cause more talk, not that it would stop him from trying.

''You know I can't do any of that,'' he said.

''Then I don't see that we have anything left to discuss. Taking this any further would be a huge mistake, a mistake I intend to avoid.'' She called to an unhappy-looking Dog, bringing him to heel. ''I suggest you get back to your side of the fence, Kincaid. And this time, stay put.''

Frustration ate at him. ''Wire can be cut, Featherstone. Fences can be torn down.''

''And what would that accomplish?'' She rescued her hat from the ground and slapped it against her thigh to remove the dust. Squashing it onto her head, she climbed aboard Tickle. ''Fences separate everything that should stay separate. Kincaids and Featherstones don't belong together. They never have. You tear down any more fences and you'll end up with worse than corrupted breeding stock.''

''Is that what our baby would be?'' he shot back. ''Corrupted breeding stock?''

He'd shocked her. Her hand slipped low on her belly cupping it in a protective gesture as old as time. ''We don't even know if there is a baby,'' she protested.

''Then I suggest you consider that possibility. Because if you're carrying my child, those fences between us are coming down. Fair warning, Raine. I'll tear them apart with my bare hands if that's what it takes to get to you and my baby. And once they're down, they're staying where they fall.''

"There's no baby," she argued.

"They're still coming down.'' The muscles along his jaw tightened, underscoring a determination driven by what he'd read in her eyes after he'd kissed her. ''You hear me, woman? No more fences. Not after last night. And not after what just happened a few minutes ago. The second you let me touch you, you opened a gate between us. I won't have you locking it against me again.''

It wasn't an idle threat and she knew it. Wheeling Tickle around, she lit out for home. But he knew she carried his words with her. Only one question remained....

Was she also carrying his baby?

CHAPTER SEVEN

RAINE answered the knock at the door and stared in surprise at Lucien. "What are you doing here?"

He leaned against the porch rail, taking up an inordinate amount of space. "Hello to you, too. Pleasant evening, wouldn't you agree?" He tilted his head back and gazed skyward. "Full moon. Cool breeze. Not too hot or cold. What could be more perfect?"

"Okay, now I know something's wrong."

"What makes you say that?"

She snapped on the outside light and got her first good look at him. What she saw had her thrusting open the door and joining him on the porch. She reached up and tilted his chin to one side, clicking her tongue in dismay. "Good heavens, Kincaid. What happened to you?"

"Nothing."

She ran a gentle finger across the bruised arch of his cheekbone. "Are you all right?"

He captured her hand in his. "It's nothing," he repeated.

"It doesn't look like nothing. It looks like you slammed your eye into someone's fist."

"I might have done something that stupid," he conceded.

She released her breath in an exasperated sigh and tugged her hand free of his. "Please tell me this doesn't involve either you playing the great protector, or a big-mouthed jerk named Buster."

His brows drew together in mock thoughtfulness. "Now that you mention it, the name does ring a bell."

"Let me guess. He said something that involved our night together at the line shack and you felt obligated to break his nose again."

"Obligation...pleasure." Lucien shrugged. "What can I say? The man clearly has a death wish. Though last time it was my nose that got broken. This time it was his."

Excessive satisfaction threaded his voice, suggesting it wasn't just Buster's nose that had taken a battering. Thank goodness Lucien wasn't a cat. Otherwise he'd have dragged over his half-dead prey to show off what a wonderful hunter he was. That's all she needed—a bent and mangled Buster oozing all over her front porch while Lucien roared in triumph.

"Well, at least you didn't end up in jail again," she said, determined to look at the bright side.

"Yet."

She peeked around him. "Should I be on the lookout for the Sheriff Tilson? Do you need a place to hide out?"

His mouth curved upward. "I think we're safe."

"I'm relieved to hear it. Although, I must say, you seem pretty calm for a man who's on the lam from the law."

He leaned forward, invading her space. "I think the more interesting observation is where I've chosen to spend my few remaining hours of freedom."

Uh-oh. She thought they'd settled this a full week ago. Judging by the angle of his jaw, she was sadly mistaken. "What's up, Kincaid?" She folded her arms across her chest. "Why are you here?"

He unknotted her arms and drew her to a pair of rockers decorating the porch. "I have news about Old Bullet."

"And I need to sit down to hear it?"

"To hear about that…and other things."

He had her comfortably situated in one of the chairs before she could think of an excuse to refuse. How did he do that? It was a talent she wouldn't mind acquiring. "Okay, I'm sitting. What did you find out?"

He sank into the rocker next to hers and lifted one huge foot to the porch railing. Giving an easy shove, he sent the chair in motion. "One of my men was responsible for what happened to your animal. A kid named Rand."

"He was at the line shack the day after the storm, wasn't he?"

"The one who kept staring at you, yeah. That's him. I kicked him off Kincaid land and made arrangements to replace your bull."

"That's not necessary."

"It is necessary."

She could tell from his tone that she wouldn't be winning this particular battle. "Is that it? You came all this way to tell me you'd beaten the hell out of Buster, fired one of your wranglers and would be buying me a replacement Bullet?"

"There's one or two more topics we have to discuss." He looked at her. The porch light fell across his face, capturing the intense darkness of his eyes and chasing the shadows from the sculpted angles of cheekbone, brow, and chin. "Like…. How's our baby?"

Her chair squeaked to a stop. "Come again?"

"Our baby. Is there one?"

Her mouth had gone bone dry and she shot a wild-eyed glance toward the front door. Nanna might have guessed what had happened at that line shack, but Raine would just as soon not have Lucien confirm it. Didn't he know how that bass rumble of his carried in the night air?

"I have no idea whether I'm pregnant," she whispered. "And I'd appreciate it if you'd not broadcast our misdeeds to all and sundry."

"By sundry, I assume you mean your grandmother. I've got news for you, honey. If you think Nanna's in the dark about what went on between us, you're kidding yourself. But I'll keep it down, if it makes you feel better." He lowered his voice to bedroom level, which almost had her sliding out of her chair. "Is it too soon to tell about the baby?"

"Yes. Plus—" She broke off, not sure she wanted to explain her other problem.

"Plus, what?"

This had to be one of the most uncomfortable conversations she'd ever conducted. "Think about it, Lucien," she said. "I can't exactly walk into the local drugstore and pick up a pregnancy test. People would talk. And it's not like I have one lying around."

"I hadn't considered that." His chair continued its gentle rock. "Tell you what. I'll call a place out of town and arrange to have one mailed to you. Would that work?"

"Yeah. It'll work. Thanks."

"No problem." There was another lag in the conversation and this time she knew he'd leave. Sure enough, he released his breath in a rough sigh. "I should go. But I'll drop in again tomorrow."

"Tomorrow?"

He lifted an eyebrow. "You have an objection?"

"Don't get your skivvies in a bunch," she attempted

to placate. "I just wondered why you'd need to stop by again."

"Didn't I mention?" He ran a hand across his jaw. "Huh. Thought I had."

He was driving her insane and it was deliberate. She knew it. He knew it. The entire state of Texas probably knew it. "Told me…what, Kincaid?" she gritted out.

He shrugged. "That I plan to come calling."

"Calling." She shook her head in confusion. "I don't understand. Calling for what?"

"Not what. Who." He stood and approached her chair. Planting his hands on the armrests, he leaned in until his face was inches from hers. "I'm going to come calling as in courting calling."

"Courting." The word sounded strange on her tongue. Alien. Or maybe it was simply that her brain had short-circuited with Lucien looming over her. His electricity must have fried her electricity which explained all the tingles and brain malfunctions and tacky drooling. "You mean, dating?"

"Call it what you want." He tilted his head to one side. "Though I've always liked hearing it referred to as courting and calling. It has a nice, old-fashioned ring, don't you think?"

"Old-fashioned. Sure, Kincaid." His lips were almost touching hers. All she had to do was shift her weight forward a tiny bit and the rocker would do the rest. She'd tumble smack-dab into his mouth. "Old-fashioned certainly describes our relationship so far."

He frowned, easing back just as she eased forward. "It does from now on. This time I'm going to get it right. Anyway, I just thought I'd stop by and let you know that was my intention."

She casually scooted closer. "We followed this path

once before and discovered it doesn't lead anywhere. Remember?''

"I'm persistent. I want to try the path again.''

She leaned forward one final inch and almost fell out of the chair as he stepped back. "Persistent, huh?'' she muttered.

"That's me. Mr. Take-Advantage-of-Every-Opportunity.'' He actually ruffled her hair. "Do me a favor after I leave and give Junior's mom a kiss for me.''

He was grinning as he crossed the porch, the rat. Clattering down the steps, he climbed into his pickup, leaving her without the last word, a last kiss or the least idea how to douse the fire he'd ignited. She scowled, kicking the rocking chair into motion again.

When had she become such a pushover? After swearing she didn't want anything further to do with him, the minute he came within an inch of her she was ready to surrender her lips. Heck, she was ready to swan dive into his arms. And he knew it. Courting, in a pig's eye. He just wanted to torture her by bringing his mouth over and then not sharing it.

Nanna joined her on the porch just as Lucien's pickup disappeared down the drive. "Was that Lucien's voice I heard?''

"Yeah.'' Raine cleared her throat. Her voice sounded odd, soft and mushy and—heaven help her—tender. "You just missed him.''

"What did he want?''

"He came calling.''

Nanna was faster on the uptake than Raine had been. "Calling calling or courting calling?''

"The courting sort.''

Nanna took the news calmly, only a suspicious glitter in her eyes betraying her amusement. "In that case, I better go shopping tomorrow and pick up some apples and lemons.''

Raine frowned. ''I tell you Lucien's going to call on me and you have to buy apples and lemons? What am I missing?''

Nanna clicked her tongue. ''I thought I raised you better, girl. A man comes courting and you'd better have a good supply of lemonade and apple pie on hand.''

''Ah. A courting rule, is it?''

''More of a law, I'd say.''

Raine buried a grin. Unless something had changed in the past decade, Lucien was going to hate this particular law every bit as much as he hated lemonade. ''One suggestion, Nanna.''

''What's that, pigeon?''

''Lucien takes his lemonade like his women.''

Nanna's brows shot up. ''Which is?''

''Extra tart.''

Lucien joined Raine on the porch, accepting the brimming glass of lemonade she offered without hardly wincing at all. He manfully downed a healthy swig of the stuff, same as he had every other night for the past week. And just like very other night his mouth puckered up so tight it was a wonder he didn't swallow his teeth.

It took close to five minutes before the tears cleared and the sensation returned to his tongue. ''You did tell Nanna that she didn't have to go to all this trouble, I hope?'' he gasped out.

''No trouble at all,'' Raine replied cheerfully. ''She insisted on fixing it for you. I'll have you know she squeezes all those lemons with her own two hands, day after day. For hours on end she sits in that kitchen, squeezing lemons. Just. For. You. There aren't many people she'd take the trouble to please like that. She must have a soft spot for you."

If his tongue weren't curled into a painful ball, he'd have begged for mercy. As it was, he summoned a look of gratitude and choked down another mouthful. It took five more agonizing minutes before he could speak again. "So, how was your day?"

"There's still a fence separating me from my property, so I guess my day wasn't as good as it might have been."

He took the complaint in stride, knowing she did it to fortify the barriers separating them. She also did it to hide the ache gnawing at her, an ache that gnawed at him every bit as fiercely. "Feel free to crawl over that fence anytime you have a hankering to visit."

"Too risky. Barbed wire leaves scars."

"I'll protect you. Just say the word and I'll be happy to help you over that fence."

"Think I'll pass, thanks." She picked up the pitcher of lemonade resting on the table between them and aimed it toward his glass. "Shall I top you off?"

He jerked his glass clear of danger. "Only if you want to die." Dead silence filled the air. Aw, hell. Had he said that out loud? He must have. Before he had time to spit out an apology, he caught her smothered laugh and straightened in the rocker. "Son of a— You know I hate lemonade, don't you? You do remember."

"I have no idea what you're talking about."

"The hell you don't." He chucked the last of his lemonade over the railing and into the nearest flowerbed. Then he stood, lifted Raine out of her chair and sat down again with her on his lap. "Woman, I will get even for that. My tongue is so blistered it's a wonder I can form words."

She grinned. ''That's the price you pay when you come calling without asking permission first.'' Her voice dropped an octave and assumed a drawl remarkably similar to his. '''Didn't I mention? Huh. Thought I had. I plan to come calling.' How generous of you to give me a choice in the matter.''

Time to exact a small revenge. He cupped a hand over her abdomen, spreading his fingers wide. ''So, how's Junior?''

He absorbed the instantaneous kick of her reaction. A delicious shudder rippled through her while a feminine heat filled his palm. ''You don't listen very well, do you?'' she retorted. Calm. Cool. And collected. He had to give her credit. If he hadn't felt the intensity of her reaction, he'd never have picked up on it in her voice. ''I've told you a hundred times that there is no Junior. I'm not pregnant, Lucien.''

''You sure?''

''As positive as I can be without taking a test.''

''You know how I can always tell when you're lying?''

Her breath escaped in a soft rush. ''How?''

''Your chin juts out.''

''Yours does that when you're being Mr. Tough Guy.'' She dropped her head to his shoulder. ''Poor Junior. Between the two of us, he doesn't stand a chance, does he?''

''Doesn't look like it.'' He waited a minute before adding, ''Do me a favor and take that test.''

She curled deeper into his embrace. ''Is that why you've come calling, as you like to phrase it? Because you're waiting to see if I'm pregnant? Getting a foot in the door just in case?''

He couldn't see her expression any longer, but something in her posture warned that she was feeling vulnerable. "I'm here because I want to be," he stated evenly. "I'm here because we belong together and I'm hoping that, given time, you'll realize that, too."

"At the risk of ticking you off, it's just lust, Lucien. That's all it's ever been."

He didn't allow her words to anger him. He knew when he heard fear speaking, and it was doing more than speaking. It was screaming. He swept her hair back from her brow, allowing the thick strands to flow through his fingers. "Lust is part of it," he admitted. "But what I'm feeling is a damn sight more than mere lust. I want you, Raine. I want every bit of you. Your intelligence. Your spirit. Your way with animals. Your generosity and plain-speaking and capacity for love. And I'll take you whether you're pregnant or not."

"What if the test is positive?"

He gathered her close, feathering a kiss along her temple. "I think the more interesting question is… What if it's negative?"

Raine slipped downstairs in her stockinged feet, carrying her hat, her boots and the keys to her Jeep. Padding quietly behind came Dog. He kept close to her heels, no doubt concerned at the possibility of being left behind. Not that it would happen. She could use his companionship.

As soon as she reached the mudroom, she shoved her feet into her boots and jammed her Stetson on top of her head. She hadn't even taken the time to braid her hair and it skimmed her shoulders, swirling heavily to her hips. Right now her only concern was to escape the house and drive out beneath the stars. To breathe and think…and worry.

The door had long ago rusted shut on the stripped-down Jeep and she slung a leg over the driver's side and climbed behind the steering wheel. Without a roof or canvas topping, the moon and stars were able to accompany her on the drive. Firing up the engine, she eased down a road that was scarcely more than a rutted path. It ran through heavy brush, climbing hillocks and roaming around deep ridges before dead-ending on a bluff at the eastern edge of Featherstone property. Parking, she switched off the lights. The first breath of dawn eased the heavy darkness from the nighttime sky, allowing her to see the lush valley stretched out below her. In the center stood a rambling ranch house and a number of smaller buildings. They all belonged to the same man.

Lucien Kincaid.

She leaned back in her seat and closed her eyes. Too bad she couldn't shut out the man as easily as she could the view. "So what now, Dog?" she asked the animal seated alertly beside her.

With a high-pitched whine, he pawed at her leg, forcing her to respond to him.

She opened one eye. "I don't want to hear it," she argued. "There's no point in talking this over with Lucien. He doesn't talk things over. He doesn't discuss. He doesn't debate. What he does is issue orders."

Dog growled softly.

"I'm not being stubborn. I'm being practical. Why do you think I've never married before this?" A sharp bark greeted the question and she turned on the animal. "You take that back! I am not in love with Lucien. I never married because I wanted someone special. A soul mate. With two regrettable exceptions, I've spent my entire life being practical and responsible. When I marry I want the fairy tale. And that's not Lucien Kincaid."

She didn't care for the expression on Dog's hairy little face, any more than she cared for the tone of his growl. "You're delusional, you sorry excuse for a border collie. Lucien isn't some sort of knight in shining armor. He's every bit as practical and responsible as I am. Throw in a good dose of ruthlessness, bullheaded tenacity and—" At Dog's sneeze, she lifted her hands in surrender. "Okay, fine. Ruthlessness, bullheaded tenacity and hot sex. But when we're not making love, we'll spend our lives arguing. How could you wish that on me?"

She could have sworn Dog laughed. At least, it sure sounded like a laugh.

"No, you miserable cow hound," she bit out. "You can wish all the hot sex on me you want. I meant, how could you wish the other stuff on me? The stuff that constantly has us at odds."

To her surprise, Dog didn't respond. Instead, he tensed in his seat, his attention fixed on Lucien's ranch house. After a moment, his ears perked forward and he lunged against the dash, barking hysterically.

"Where?" She jerked around to stare at the Kincaid homestead. "I don't see it."

With a desperate howl, Dog leapt from the Jeep and shot beneath the fence, streaking down the hillside. Raine's heart thundered in her chest and for a full second she couldn't force herself to move. All she could do was pray Dog was wrong. After what seemed an eternity, her muscles finally cooperated. Swiveling, she reached into the back and grabbed a small toolbox resting on the floor behind her. Snapping it open, she dumped the contents on the passenger seat. The wire cutters were the last to tumble from the box.

Raine snatched them up and vaulted over the door of the Jeep, running for the fence blocking her access to

Kincaid land. It only required a few minutes to snip the fence, though it seemed to take forever. Without gloves, the barbs sank into her hands, tearing the skin. Not that she cared. There were times when desperation overrode pain and this was one of them.

Finished, she jumped into the Jeep and gunned it, screaming through the break in the fence. There wasn't a road down the hillside, not even a path. Wrapping her bleeding hands around the steering wheel, she forged on. On the seat beside her the tools rattled together in a discordant objection. Half scattered onto the floor, the other half bounced over the open side of the Jeep. On a particularly vicious curve, the toolbox sailed out the back, banging along in her wake.

Thick brush bashed against the front of the Jeep, shattering the headlights and making it impossible to see trouble before she ran into it. And on two separate occasions she nearly rolled the ancient vehicle. It tipped back onto all four wheels at the last instant, flattening a tire each time. How she managed to avoid a nasty wreck, she never knew. With two of her tires gone, steering was next to impossible. A hundred feet from the ranch house she took out the front corner panel against an inconveniently placed cottonwood. The instant she reached the floor of the valley, she stomped full on the gas petal and didn't let up until she'd practically driven the thing onto Lucien's porch. It ground to a gasping halt, steam hissing from beneath the hood.

Leaping from her seat, she pelted up the steps and banged on the locked door. Dog reached the ranch house just behind her. She could smell the smoke now, though she couldn't see any flames. No one came in response to her hammering and Dog threw himself against the door, scratching and barking frantically. Raine knew he wouldn't do that unless Lucien were still in the house.

There wasn't any time to spare. Grabbing one of the rockers from the porch, she heaved it in an arcing semicircle and smashed it against one of the two huge plate-glass windows book-ending the door. The glass shattered, razor-sharp shards raining down both inside the house and out. Carefully stepping over the sill, she paused in the entryway.

"Lucien!" she shouted. "Where are you?"

A terrifying silence met her call, thick and stifling and deadly. Smoke was rapidly filling the house and she could hear the first crackle of a nearby fire. She had to find Lucien, and fast.

"Dog, get help," she ordered.

She didn't wait to see if he obeyed. She knew the collie wouldn't let her down. Three different directions branched off from the foyer where she stood—one to the left toward large, high-ceiling rooms, one to the right toward the kitchen area, and a staircase upward. A light beckoned from the right. Whatever she decided next could determine whether or not she got to Lucien in time. Taking a deep breath, she followed her instincts. She ignored the light and plunged up the staircase toward what she hoped would be the bedrooms.

The smoke was thicker the further she climbed and her shouts turned to a coughing fit. Stripping off her blouse, she tied it around her face. An instant later, she tripped over Lucien. He lay, facedown, near the top of the steps.

Not wasting any time, she grabbed two fistfuls of his shirt and fought to pull him closer to the edge. It was slow going. He was like a sack of wet concrete, almost impossible to maneuver. He stirred just as she gained the first step.

"Wake up, Kincaid!" She shoved back her hair, using the full power of her voice. "Move it, you lousy claim jumper. We need to get out of here."

He groaned in response. "Not a claim jumper." His response came slow and slurred, not that she cared. Having him argue with her was the sweetest sound she'd ever heard.

"You have to help, Lucien. You're too heavy for me to carry. Can you sit up?" When he didn't respond, she shook him, pushing every ounce of persuasive power she possessed into her words. "Sit up, Kincaid. Now!"

With a groan, he grabbed at the banister and pulled himself upright. "Bossy woman."

"File a complaint with someone who gives a hot damn."

Having Lucien sitting at the top of the steps was all the help she needed. Wrapping her arms around him, she allowed their combined weight to carry them down the wooden treads on their backsides. They bounced with bone-bruising speed over the dozen or more steps to the bottom. A painful meeting with the stone foyer floor ended their descent and a leather-bound work journal slipped from Lucien's waistband. She gathered it up and thrust it beneath her own belt. Clearly it was important or he wouldn't have risked his life to go after it.

"Lucien? Come on, sweetheart. We have to get out of here."

He didn't respond, not to the demand, nor the endearment. She eyed the door, fighting the first stirring of panic. Unconscious or not, she had to get him out of the house. She tried to stand, a wrenching pain in her knee warning that she'd twisted something. Badly. She set her chin. If she couldn't stand, then she'd crawl. But one way or another, she was getting out of this house and she was taking Lucien with her.

Inch by inch she dragged the two of them toward the door. It crashed inward when she was halfway there and a dozen men poured across the threshold. Two of them grabbed her and the rest wrestled Lucien's bulk out of the door. An instant later they reached the grassy expanse of yard and she ripped the covering from around her face and gulped in the sweet, fresh air. Rolling over, she scrambled on hands and knees to Lucien's side.

His men ringed them, their expressions frighteningly somber. To her surprise, Rand was among them. "What's wrong with him?" she asked.

Dobey crouched next to her. "Somebody knocked his ears down." He picked up her crumpled shirt from off the ground and helped her into it. "He's out cold and there's a lump the size of Texas decorating his skull."

"He's not going to—" Her voice broke and tears welled into her eyes.

"Ambulance is on its way," was all the foreman would say.

Raine swiped away tears with the back of her hand. Their relationship was not going to end this way. It wasn't fair. Not after all they'd been through. Grabbing the front of Lucien's shirt she bent close. "Don't you die on me, you ornery son of a bitch," she ordered. "Don't you dare. Our baby needs a father. You hear me, Kincaid? Junior needs you!"

CHAPTER EIGHT

JUNIOR needs you!

It was like moving through a vat of molasses—slow, sticky and as uncomfortable as hell. Everything ached. His chest. His head. Damn, even his tailbone felt like it had been drop-kicked. Slowly Lucien pried his eyes open and winced at the bright lights.

You hear me, Kincaid? Junior needs you!

The demand rang in his ears, more insistent this time, and overriding every other hurt. Taking a deep breath— even that proved a challenge—he sat straight up in bed. His breath escaped in a half gasp, half groan and it took every ounce of willpower not to collapse back against the pillow. When his head cleared and the room stopped spinning in a slow circle, he looked around.

Oh, man, this couldn't be good. Circling him like a string of electronic ponies were tubes and wires and every sort of hospital-ish gadget, all of which were tethered directly to him. He winced, his head pounding out an endless refrain.

Don't you die on me, you ornery son of a bitch! Don't you dare. Our baby needs a father. You hear me, Kincaid? Junior needs you!

Junior? The fire! There'd been smoke and a fire. And then Raine had somehow showed up. And she'd said…Junior! With a roar designed to cover the pain, he ripped himself free of the various lassos restraining him and escaped the bed.

He swayed in place as the air surrounding him turned

into a turbulent ocean. It crashed against his chest and swirled around his legs, almost succeeding in sweeping him to the floor. He fought against the lift and drag for an endless moment before finding his feet and getting them properly situated beneath him. For the first time ever, he was grateful they were so big. He needed every available inch to maintain his balance.

No sooner had he cleared most of the fog bank from his head and gained control of his various limbs when two nurses appeared in the doorway. The first, clearly the more senior of the two, stared at him in outraged horror.

"Mr. Kincaid! What are you doing?"

"I'd think that was obvious."

His voice rasped in his throat, cutting like shards of glass. A plastic pitcher of water stood on a stand near his bed. He snatched it up, ripped off the lid and emptied half the contents in a single gulp. Fresh, icy water cascaded down his throat, tasting like liquid heaven. He dumped the remains of the pitcher—mostly ice—over his head and bellowed half in pain, half in pleasure. Fully awake now, he tossed the pitcher aside and shook the slush from his wet hair. His impromptu shower had cleared the remaining wisps of fog blanketing his brain. It had also lowered the volume on the jackhammers ratcheting away in his skull.

The senior nurse didn't look pleased. "If you want water or a bath, we'd be happy to help you with both."

"Too late. I just took care of it for you. Now I'm getting the hell out of here."

"I'm sorry, Mr. Kincaid. You can't do that."

"Watch me." He squinted until he could make out her name tag. "Ms. Strum."

"You have a possible concussion, not to mention

smoke inhalation. You can't leave until the doctor approves your discharge.''

"Sure I can. All I have to do is put one foot in front of the other until I get to the door marked Exit. I then plan to avail myself of your door's kind offer and exit my backside out of here.'' He rubbed a hand across his bewhiskered jaw. "I'm guessing it's a straight shot from there, wouldn't you agree?''

She lifted an eyebrow. "You're going to leave dressed in a hospital gown?''

Her acerbic question set his head to pounding again. "Where are my clothes?''

"Not here.'' She folded her arms across her ample chest and smiled as though she thought she'd won the argument. Fool woman. "Once the doctor releases you, we'll return them.''

He changed tactics. "What happened to Raine?''

The younger nurse peeked out from behind her supervisor. He could just make out a tag pinned to her uniform with the name Shirl typed across it in large block letters. "Are you talking about Raine Featherstone?'' she asked.

Nurse Rules-and-Regs cut her off. "We're not allowed to give out information on other patients unless you're family.''

Behind her, Shirl winked and gave him the thumbs-up. Even with his aching head he understood that to mean Raine was okay. "Was she injured?'' he demanded.

"I told you, we can't release that information without the patient's permission,'' the older nurse repeated.

Again Shirl peeked out, shaking her head no. With a frown Nurse Strum whipped around. In that split second Shirl's expression went from sly to wide-eyed and dumb-as-a-brick. If he hadn't been afraid he'd pass out from the pain, he'd have laughed out loud. Spinning back to face Lucien, Strum pointed to the bed. "You. Get in."

It was the wrong tact to take with him. "I don't respond well to orders, sweetcakes," he rumbled a warning. "And I'm not getting back into bed. What I am going to do is bust out of here and that's with clothes or without them."

She stared in patent disbelief. "You'd leave half naked?"

Did she doubt him? "Half naked, whole naked, or crawling on hands and knees. Doesn't matter much to me. And if you think I won't, prepare yourself for a show." He yanked at the snarl of knots holding his hospital gown in place. When they didn't immediately give, he simply ripped the gown from stem to stern. "One way or another I'm going after my woman. Unless you have a serious death wish, I suggest you stand clear of my trail."

With that, he allowed the shredded hospital gown to drop to the floor. Stripping the sheet from the bed—and gamely suppressing a groan in the process—he wrapped the blasted thing around his waist. Been there, done this. Doing it again couldn't be any more embarrassing than the first go-round. When he next looked up a wall of jabbering nurses blocked the doorway. Where the hell had they come from?

"What the devil do you think you're doing, Kincaid?" a voice came from behind the wall. "I leave you alone for two minutes and you start a commotion."

"Raine?"

"Who else would it be?"

She was somewhere at the back of the pack and he

glared at the mob of women standing between him and the most important part of his life. "Make a hole!"

They practically tripped over themselves in an effort to clear a path. The minute an opening formed, Raine limped into the room. Catching a glimpse of his getup, she grinned. "You naked in a sheet. Just like old times, huh, Kincaid? No wonder you collected an audience." She shooed everyone from the room, with the unfortunate exception of Strum. "It's downright pitiful what the sight of a naked man will do to a woman, even when his miserable hide's as scarred up as yours. We're going to need a mop to clean up all this drool."

His gaze locked with hers, practically eating her alive. "You okay?"

"Fine."

"You're limping."

"An old football injury."

This time he did laugh. It was every bit as painful as he'd feared. Maybe even more so. "What do you say we bust out of this jail?" he asked once he could breathe again. "You game?"

To his relief, she didn't fight him. He wasn't sure he could have lasted even half a round if she had. "Get his clothes," she barked at Strum. "We're leaving."

"Not until he signs a paper stating that he's checking out against medical advice." The nurse planted her fists on hips the size of a linebacker's shoulders. "One signature in exchange for one pair of jeans. Take it or leave it."

Lucien didn't waste any time accepting the compromise. Strum was a feisty old bird, he'd give her that. But even feisty old birds could be pushed only so far before they called in younger reinforcements. "Done," he agreed.

It still took longer than he liked to make good their escape. By the time the staff had loaded him down with a stack of papers containing dire warnings and predictions, and added every verbal threat imaginable on top of it, he could barely set one foot in front of the other. Fortunately, he didn't have to. An orderly showed up, pushing a wheelchair. He wanted to fall to his knees in gratitude. He covered the pitiful lapse in manliness by grumbling out a complaint.

To his secret amusement, Raine didn't let him get away with it. "Yeah, yeah. We know how tough you are, Kincaid. Hospital regulations be damned, real men don't ride anything that doesn't wear horseshoes. And you feel so good you could single-handedly wrastle, rope, and brand every last cow on your ranch."

"Maybe not wrastle. But I sure as hellfire could rope and brand the lot of 'em."

She shoved him into the wheelchair. "Oh, sit down and shut up before I toss your carcass back in that bed where it belongs."

Deciding silence would serve him best at this point, he didn't bother racking his muddled brain for a comeback guaranteed to be more witless than witty. He held his tongue until they were outside beneath the excessive benevolence of a Texas sun. The orderly dropped him off by Nanna's car, before departing. Lucien regarded it with cautious admiration. The car was a huge old sedan that could have locked horns with Old Bullet and come out the winner.

"Where's your rust bucket?" he asked.

She opened the passenger door for him. "If you mean my Jeep, it died a nasty death in the arms of your front porch." He eyed the driver's side and she shook her

head. "Don't even think about it, Kincaid. I'm not risking my hide just to salvage your masculine pride."

"Nor risk our baby's well-being?" The question escaped like a shot.

She didn't duck it, but met his gaze squarely. "Nor
Junior's."

For some reason he had trouble unlocking his jaw.
"Then you're really pregnant?"

"That's what your test says. And it's what all six of
mine have confirmed." She inclined her head toward the
car. "Get in, Lucien. We can talk about it on the way."

He didn't need any further prompting. He eased himself into the car and waited with a notable lack of patience while she circled to the driver's side and climbed
in. "When did you find out?"

"The day of the fire."

"This morning?"

She fired the engine before answering. "Day before
yesterday."

Two days? Was she joking? "Are you telling me I've
been in the hospital the past forty-eight hours?" He
couldn't believe it. "No wonder they weren't in any
hurry to let me leave."

"You've even been awake on and off, although the
doctor said you probably wouldn't remember. Somebody
scrambled your eggs, but good."

"The doctor's right. I don't remember."

"None of it?" She spared him a quick glance as she
pulled out of the parking lot. "What about the fire?"

"I remember that." Another memory surfaced. "I
also remember you called me a son of a bitch."

She looked amused. "Figures."

"You ordered me not to die." He honed in on the

main topic of his concern. "You said our baby needed a father."

A hint of color swept along her cheekbones and she kept her gaze fixed out the front windshield. "She does. He does."

"Does Nanna know?"

She released a gusty sigh. "We weren't alone when I told you. I pretty much announced it to the entire world." Her lips twitched. "Dobey almost passed out right beside you. 'Course that could have been because I wasn't wearing my shirt."

He blinked. "You want to run that by me again?"

"I'd taken off my shirt and wrapped it around my face because the smoke was so thick." A hint of defensiveness crept into her voice. "It was either that or not breathe."

This was ridiculous. He needed to have a serious talk with her and it wasn't going to happen during the brief drive back to their respective ranches, especially if she planned to go out of her way to keep the conversation light and amusing. Not that he minded light and amusing. But right now he needed serious and practical. "Pull over, will you?"

Shooting him a look of concern, she eased Nanna's tank to the side of the road. "Are you sick?"

"It's not that. We have to talk and I'd rather do it where we won't be overheard."

Her grip tightened around the steering wheel. It was a telling gesture. Even a man with scrambled eggs could see she'd rather duck this particular conversation. "I'll give you ten minutes to speak your mind," she offered. "After that I have orders to get you tucked up in bed."

Didn't she understand? "I don't give a damn what that hospital said. You and I are long past a bit of plain speaking, sweetheart. We have some decisions to make and I intend to see to it that they're not just made, but that the two of us are officially signed, sealed, and delivered, not to mention wedded and fully bedded." He couldn't resist adding a testosterone driven, "Or should I say, bedded again."

A smile quivered at the corners of her mouth. "It wasn't the hospital issuing the ten minute moratorium," she explained gently. "That comes from a higher authority."

It didn't take much guesswork to figure out whose. "Nanna?"

"She's made up the guest room for you and I'm to inform you that you'll be staying with us for a while. That should give us plenty of time for all that signing and sealing. As for the wedding and bedding, that's not a ten-minute conversation and you know it."

"Probably not even a twenty minute one." The jackhammers had started burrowing into his skull again. "There's only one small problem. I'm staying at my place, not yours. Tell Nanna thanks, but no thanks."

Her breath escaped in an irritated sigh. "You don't listen very well, do you, Kincaid? Smoke. Fire. Bashed head. You don't have a 'your' place anymore. The kitchen is pretty much gutted and the rest of the house has serious smoke damage. It's going to take months to get the place repaired."

"No problem. I can bunk in with my men."

"You could, except—"

Hell's bells. He ran a hand across his jawline. It was a serious mistake. Two days worth of beard did its level best to scrape the skin off. It would have, too, if he didn't have so many calluses protecting his palm. "Let me guess. Nanna got hold of my men."

"You won't be going anywhere until Nanna's good and ready to let you. She warned your entire payroll that she'd skin them alive if you snuck within spitting distance of your property anytime in the next week. And she'd toast them like marshmallows if you tried spreading your bedroll in the bunkhouse."

"Well, then. I guess I'll say, 'Thank you, ma'am, I appreciate your hospitality.'"

"That's about all you'll get to say."

He deliberately turned the conversation in the direction of a more urgent interest. "How upset is she about the baby?"

"Oh, Nanna's thrilled about the baby." Raine grimaced. "She's not nearly as happy about the order in which recent events have transpired. Babies, I've been told in no uncertain terms, are the caboose on a train, not its engine."

"You have to admit, she's got the right of it." He couldn't blame Nanna for being upset. This couldn't be the way she'd planned to become a great-grandmother. To be honest, it wasn't how he'd planned to become a father, either. When it came to babies, he was strictly a wedding-bells-first kind of guy. "I don't suppose she'll cut me any slack until I've had time to recover?"

"Not a chance."

"Somehow I didn't think so."

Raine swiveled to face him, planting her back against the driver side door and drawing her legs up close to her chest. "Before we discuss the baby, I need to ask you about something else."

"Shoot."

"How much do you remember about the events preceding the fire?"

"A fair amount."

"Then there's something you should know." She wrapped her arms around her legs and rested her chin on her knees. "It's about that kid you fired. Rand. The one who shot Old Bullet."

"What about him?"

"Sheriff Tilson arrested him for setting your place on fire."

Lucien straightened in his seat. "Aw, hell. That's not what happened."

"That's what Rand claims, but I had the impression he wasn't holding out much hope that you'd vouch for him."

"'Course I'll vouch for him." He hesitated, compelled to confide in her. "I think he might be my brother."

Raine stared in disbelief. "Come again?"

"The kid claims he's my half brother. That Dad had an affair with his mother shortly before my parents divorced. He hired on because he wanted to get to know me."

Her disbelief turned to outrage. "So, shooting my bull was just for kicks? Boyish high jinks to impress big brother?"

"Frustration is more like it. After twenty years, he's grown himself a good-size patch of resentment. He'd never worked on a ranch before hiring on with me. And all he could talk about was how his life would have been different if our father had acknowledged him. That he'd have gotten to share in what I now enjoy. He thinks I knew who he was and deliberately assigned him the toughest stretch of fence to ride, so I'd have an excuse to fire him."

She dismissed Rand's assertion out of hand. "That's ridiculous. You'd never do something like that."

"That's what I told him. Not that he believes me. What he doesn't realize is that even if he'd lived with Dad, he wouldn't have been raised on a ranch. Dad escaped for the city as soon as he was old enough to hitch a ride."

"While you did just the opposite."

Lucien nodded. "I arrived on my grandparents' doorstep at the ripe old age of ten and announced that the only way they'd get rid of me was to sell me to the circus. I'm not quite sure, but I think I was half hoping they'd take me up on my offer."

Raine chuckled. "Odd, isn't it? Your parents hated ranch life while mine adored it. If they hadn't died in that car wreck, they'd have stepped in after Paps died."

The shadow of her grandfather crept between them again. It was a shadow he'd do anything to eradicate. "Honey—"

She stopped him before he had a chance to say anything else. "It's time we made our peace about Paps, Lucien." Tears glittered in her eyes, tears she valiantly tried to suppress. "I don't blame you for his death. Not anymore."

He must have sucked up more smoke than he'd realized. Not only was it affecting his brain, but his throat felt tight and raw, making speech downright painful. "Why not? What's changed?"

"It was something Nanna said." The muscles in her cheek jerked, betraying the emotional turmoil hiding just beneath the calm. "She asked me how I'd have felt if you'd been the one to die that day."

"And?" The word escaped more harshly than he'd planned.

"It was a horrible thought, but it helped me face facts." Sorrow gleamed in her eyes. "I'd have forgiven him, Lucien. I'd have hated it, but I wouldn't have spent twelve years hating him for a foolish accident, even one that had taken you from me. And yet, that's what I've tried to do over Paps death. I let it part us.''

Lucien fought to reply, but it proved a fruitless battle. He bowed his head, struggling to regain his self-control.

Raine slid across the seat and into his arms. "Let it go, Lucien. Maybe in time we can talk about it. But until we're able, let's put it behind us.''

He cleared his throat, relieved to discover it worked again. "Yeah. Let's do that.''

She deliberately changed the subject. "You haven't told me how the fire started. Rand's involved in this somehow, I gather?''

He tightened his hold on her, needing to keep her close, to know that they were both safe and together, no matter how precarious that togetherness might be. "The fire. Right.'' He rested his jaw on the top of her head. "Rand dropped by after a night of carousing right about the time I was getting up to start my workday. We exchanged a few words is all. No big deal.''

She made a sound of exasperation. "Don't give me that. He attacked you, didn't he?''

"Nah. He just wanted to show me some brotherly affection.''

"With his fist?''

That might be a good question to duck. "I had some chow cooking on the stovetop. When our discussion turned…er…animated, a small fire broke out. Wouldn't have been a problem, except Rand's not all that much smaller than I am. We kept tripping over each other trying to douse it. That's when I hit my head.''

She reared back to look at him. "And did Rand help you hit your head?''

"Not even a little. I fell against the kitchen table and clocked out. When I woke, Rand was trying his level best to drag me out of there. By then the fire was beyond controlling, so I sent the kid for help while I retrieved some important papers." A frown furrowed his brow. Which reminded him... "What happened to my work journal?"

"I have it safe and sound."

Uh-oh. He forced an easy smile to his lips. "Great."

She studied him more closely than he liked. "It must have been pretty important, considering you risked your life going after it."

Vital. Not that he'd mention that small detail to her. "There was plenty of time to fetch it. Or there would have been if I hadn't gotten dizzy again and passed out. I gather that's when you showed up?"

"Your men weren't far behind."

"Did Rand go for help?"

"Yes. At least he was there when they dragged us out of the house." Raine checked her watch. "Good heavens. Look at the time. The rest of this conversation will have to wait. We need to get home before Nanna has our guts for garters."

"Not a chance. Not until we've discussed the baby." He captured her hands in his to slow her retreat, startled when she flinched, jerking free of his grasp. "What the— What's wrong? What did I do?"

"It's nothing. You surprised me, is all." She smiled brightly. "Time to go."

Was she kidding? "It's not nothing," he bit out. "Something's wrong. What is it?"

She simply shook her head, stubborn to the end. Ever so gently he grasped her wrists and eased open her hands, palms upward. What he saw had him blistering the air with every cuss word in his vocabulary. When those ran dry, he invented a few new ones.

"Real nice, Kincaid. You do realize our baby can hear you?"

"You can nag me about my language later." He stared at her hands, a tightness building in his chest. "Explain this. Now."

CHAPTER NINE

RAINE released her breath in a sigh. "It's just a few scratches."

"This isn't a few scratches," Lucien retorted. "This looks like you got into a boxing match with an angry piece of barbed wire and the barbed wire won."

"I screwed up. Forgot to wear my boxing gloves. No big deal."

"It is a big deal." She'd never seen his eyes so dark and passionate. "This is my fault, isn't it? I don't know how or why, but I'm responsible."

"Oh, for crying out loud. You kill me, Kincaid," she scoffed. "You really do. You always need to take responsibility for everything. You can't even let me have my one little success without claiming credit for it. Well, forget it. I did this. It's all mine and you can't have it."

"Honey, if this is an example of one of your successes, I'd hate to see you fail."

Her levity faded. "Failing would have been not pulling that fence down in time."

He wasn't slow on the uptake. "The fire?"

"As usual, your fence was in my way. So I moved it. Unfortunately, I never got around to putting on my gloves."

He kissed her wrists, just above the injuries. "All I seem to do is hurt you—Paps, the baby, now this. You know I'd do everything in my power to prevent that from happening, don't you?"

"I do know." She tugged her hands free. "But it's not your job to protect me."

"Sure it is."

She shook her head. "You're not listening, Kincaid. I can look out for myself. If you'd like a partner, I might go along with it. Maybe. But stop playing Prince Charming to my Sleeping Beauty. I refuse to act like some helpless princess, standing on the sidelines wringing her hands while the big, bad knight saves the day. It's just not me. Every once in a while, I prefer wearing the suit of armor and riding to the rescue. This was one of those times."

To her surprise, he accepted her comment without argument. "Okay, partner. Talk to me about where we go from here."

She didn't bother pulling her punches. "I can guess where you'd like to go and what you want once you get there."

His eyes narrowed. "Sure. Our baby. What's wrong with that?" His calm tone belied the annoyance she sensed brewing beneath the surface. "A few weeks ago marriage didn't figure into either of our plans. It might have if we'd had more time to work on our relationship. We were headed that way."

"Were we?" She wasn't willing to concede even that much.

He made a sound of irritation. "Be honest, Raine. We couldn't keep our hands off each other. After all these years and all that's happened to keep us apart, that's saying something."

She couldn't deny it. "Maybe if our situation had been different, something might have come of our affair." To her concern, he rubbed a hand across his brow, reminding her that he had no business sitting in a car attempting to resolve a problem without any easy solutions. "Come on, Lucien. Let's go home."

"Not yet." He studied her thoughtfully. "I gather marriage to me isn't high on your list of pleasurable pursuits."

She lifted an eyebrow in response. "You proposing, Kincaid?"

Something in the way she asked the question must have warned him to back off, and fast. "It's one possibility."

"A remote one."

"Look, I admit this isn't the way either of us wanted to go into a marriage."

"Not even a little."

He reached out and smoothed her hair back from her temple. He didn't immediately release her as she'd expected. Instead, his fingers sank further into her hair, penetrating deep into the thick strands. "Then we won't."

Somehow she'd lost track of the conversation. With one simple touch, he'd stolen every coherent thought from her head. She struggled to regain her balance with only limited success. "What do you mean?" she was reduced to asking.

"I mean we won't hop into a marriage because we're forced into it."

"What other reason is there?"

"Good question. Maybe that's something we ought to think about for a spell."

"Just for a spell, huh?" With a two-day growth of beard and a hint of purple ringing his eyes, he looked like death warmed over. And yet, she found him utterly irresistible. How was that possible? "And what, exactly, are your thoughts on the subject?" she asked.

His voice dropped to a suggestive rumble. "You'd be shocked at some of the thoughts I have."

"Try me."

"I have thoughts of you and me. Naked."

"Naked." She sampled the word as though it were some exotic flavor. If they'd been anywhere else, they'd be racing to see who could strip fastest. Thank heaven they were sitting in a car on a public road. She frowned. She was thanking heaven, wasn't she? "Naked might be a thought I've had once or twice, myself," she confessed.

A fierce hunger darkened his expression. "Come here."

She shook her head. "There isn't time."

"There's always time for this."

She didn't bother protesting further. Not giving herself a chance to consider the consequences of her action, she fell into him. Instantly, his mouth came down on hers and they dissolved into an embrace that melded lips and arms and legs in a frantic tangle. Nothing mattered but having him in her arms, his hands on her body and his kisses consuming her bite by delicious bite. She'd come so close to losing him. Too close. Nothing mattered after that. Not fences. Not border disputes. Not even impossible decisions about their future.

His beard rasped across her skin, setting her nerve endings on fire. She wanted that exquisite friction elsewhere—on her breasts, her belly, skimming the sensitive skin of her thighs. He whispered a suggestion in her ear, the heat of it blasting the breath from her body.

"Yes!" The word escaped as half plea, half demand. "Do that. Do it now."

"No room. Move back a little and I can—"

A loud rapping at the passenger window caused them

both to jump. To Raine's horror Sheriff Tilson stood peering through the dusty glass at them, a broad grin decorating his ruddy face. "Here I thought poor Nanna had broken down and needed rescuing, and instead I find you two, carrying on like a couple of randy teenagers. Do I need to suggest that you find a more private place if you're going to snickerdoodle?"

Lucien swore beneath his breath, taking the words right out of Raine's mouth. To her disgust, he recovered his composure with disgusting promptness. Rolling down the window, he offered the sheriff his hand. "Glad you stopped by, Tilson."

"Uh-huh. Sure you are."

Lucien grinned. "Okay, so your timing isn't so great. But at least you've saved me a phone call. I was going to give you a ring and see if you wouldn't spring that kid you have locked up. Rand."

The sheriff leaned his forearm against the roof of the car. "I gather that means he didn't set the fire at your place. He claimed as much, but I figured I'd better hold on to him until you'd confirmed it."

"Consider it confirmed."

"I've got to tell you, Lucien. The kid reminds me of somebody." Tilson hesitated. "Now that I think about it, he has a Kincaid-ish look about him."

"There's a reason for that. Just between you, me and anyone else who hasn't figured it out just by looking at the kid, I might have picked myself up another brother."

Tilson nodded sagely. "Got it. Then he was helping the morning of the fire, not hurting."

Lucien shrugged. "Helping after. Doing a bit of hurting beforehand. But now that we've settled our differences, I suspect we can keep him clear of your jail."

The sheriff grinned. "Not if he's as much of a hothead

as you are, Kincaid. I heard about your most recent fight
with Buster. You two come to blows again and I'll have
all three of you dusting my cells, your brother included.''

"Let me get this straight. I hit Buster and you arrest
Buster, me…and Rand? What's with that?''

"Gotta have a fourth for poker, don't we?'' The sheriff straightened. "You two better hightail it home before
I get a frantic call from Nanna. And don't forget to send
the missus and me an invite to the wedding now, you
hear?''

Raine leaned across the seat toward the window and
offered a dangerous smile. Here she was, thirty years old
and still being ordered home like a teenager caught neck-
ing on Lover's Lane. "If we get married we'll be sure
to do that. But we're probably going to spend a few
years living in sin first.''

Tilson chuckled. "That threat would carry more
weight if you had a different grandmother. Face it, girl.
You and Kincaid will be walking down the aisle under
your own steam or because Nanna's dragging you there
by your ears. But married you will be and long before
that baby you're carrying lets out its first bellow.''

Before she could come up with a more brilliant comeback than, "Oh, yeah?'' the sheriff had returned to his
patrol car. Beside her Lucien was busy fighting back a
laugh, offering a perfect target for her annoyance.
"Yuck it up, mister, and I'll dent the other side of your
head. See how funny you find that.''

He held up his hands in surrender. "I'm not laughing.
It hurts too much to laugh.'' He tried his best to look
pitiful. "Take me home, sweetheart. Better yet, take me
to bed.''

Instead of appearing wounded and vulnerable, he

came across as tough and wolfish and dangerous as hell. Even so, she shouldn't find his suggestion so appealing. She started the car. "Fine. I'll take you home, Kincaid, but that's the extent of my offer."

As usual, he got in the last word. "I don't know why," he grumbled beneath his breath. "Making love in a bed would be a nice change, don't you think?"

Two weeks had passed. Two infuriating, patience-eating, useless weeks and Lucien was no closer to resolving his problems with Raine than before his accident. Every time he broached a discussion about their future, she ducked it, finding urgent business elsewhere on the ranch—elsewhere being as far from him as physically possible.

He'd tried to give her time and space, at least, as much time and space as a reasonable man would allow. But he was fast approaching the limits of what he considered reasonable. If he didn't find a way around the fences she kept throwing at him, and soon, he was going to simply chuck her over his shoulder and strike out for the nearest preacher. Before he took such drastic action, there was one final option open to him. He'd talk to the only person more ornery than his bride-to-be and ask for a bit of advice.

"Nanna? Do you have a minute?"

"I always have time for you, Lucien." She shooed him toward a chair and planted a plate of cookies and a huge glass of ice-cold milk in front of him.

He stared at the plate for a long minute. "I think I've finally realized something. You can't carry on a conversation without cookies, can you?"

She offered a smile so like Raine's that it hurt. "I discovered long ago that people have trouble arguing when they have a mouth full of cookie. And they have an even harder time arguing with the one who baked them.''

''Devious old woman.''

''Not to mention smart.'' She took the chair across from him. ''If this is about moving out, I'll tell you the same thing I have for the past two weeks. You're stuck here until I say otherwise.''

He picked up a cookie. ''I assume 'otherwise' will be about the time Raine and I are married?''

''That strikes me as good a time as any.'' She fixed him with a stern gaze. ''I plan to see to it that the wedding comes before the baby.''

''Works for me. Unfortunately, I'm having less success convincing Raine. I thought we'd have plenty of opportunity to make decisions about our future.'' He polished off the cookie and reached for another. ''But she appears intent on avoiding me at every turn.''

Nanna snorted. ''Why do you think I called in the Cupid Committee?''

Time for some plain speaking. ''You know I want to marry her?''

''I'd be disappointed if you didn't.''

''And you're okay with that? Really okay, I mean.''

She studied him for an endless moment. ''This is about Paps, isn't it?''

''Yeah.''

He slowly returned the cookie to the plate. This moment was long overdue. He'd spoken to Nanna shortly after Paps had died, but she'd been too grief stricken to do more than give a cursory acceptance to his stammered apology. Lucien had grown up that long-ago morning, and it had been both fast and painful. He'd been irrevocably changed by what had happened. He'd also vowed to find a way to leave Nanna with something more than useless words. And whether she knew it or not, he'd done his best to keep that vow.

"You have no idea how sorry I am about Paps." He offered the simple truth, plain, heartfelt and unvarnished. "There's nothing I can say to change what happened, just as there's nothing I wouldn't give to go back and try."

Nanna took his hand in both of hers. "I never held that against you, Lucien. I know it was an accident."

A muscle spasmed in his cheek. "It was. But it doesn't change the fact that I took a man's life. Your man."

She continued to hold his hand and he could literally feel her compassion flowing from her hands to his. "It wasn't deliberate. It was also more Paps fault than yours. He never should have gone after you. And he sure shouldn't have gone over in a temper, toting a shotgun."

He met her gaze and saw a bone-deep understanding reflected in her eyes, a perception that shocked him. He shook his head in disbelief. "You know." His voice dropped to a hoarse whisper. "You know all of it, don't you?"

"I do."

"And you never told Raine?"

"That's not up to me. It never was. That's your job."

"No. No. Some things are better left unsaid."

Nanna inclined her head. "That's your choice. But sometimes the not saying causes more pain than the saying."

"Forget it." He dismissed the suggestion out of hand. "This isn't one of those times."

Nanna released her breath in a long sigh. "What am I going to do about you?" She shoved another cookie into his hand as she considered her words. "Do you think I can't see the Do Not Trespass signs you've thrown up? I'm no fool. You've boarded, nailed and even strung wire to keep everyone out. Now you know my granddaughter. How do you think she's going to react when she sees the work you've put into defending your secret?"

It didn't take any thought. Raine was nothing if not consistent. "She's going to scratch herself to pieces climbing over wire and pulling off boards just so she can find out what I'm hiding."

"You got it. There's only one way to keep her from going to all that trouble. I suggest you tell her straight before she ends up with her heart broke uncovering the truth."

"All of it?"

Nanna nodded, a hint of sorrow darkening her eyes. "Even if it means telling her my part in it." She pushed out a smile. "You want to marry my granddaughter? Then one of you has to be the first to tear down the fences separating you. You strike me as the perfect man for the job."

A soft rustling woke Raine and she rolled over, struggling to peer through the gloom. "Dog?" she called.

"Not Dog." The mattress sagged under Lucien's weight and an instant later he joined her beneath the covers. Shock held her still, which no doubt worked to his advantage. "Move over a little, will you?"

"Have you lost your mind?" When she didn't immediately shift to one side, he slid his hands beneath her and forced the issue. His hands burned through the thin cotton of her nightshirt, touching where he shouldn't, yet where she secretly longed to feel his caress. "What do you think you're doing?" she demanded.

A soft laugh gusted against her temple. "Okay. Now that's the sort of question a woman of your years shouldn't have to ask." Settling beside her, he wrapped his arms around her waist and spooned her against his bare chest. "Not to mention a woman in your condition."

She sank into his warmth, barely suppressing a groan of pleasure. "Would you please be serious?"

"I've been trying to get serious with you for two full weeks." A hint of censure colored his words. "You've been avoiding me. And it's been deliberate."

"So make an appointment," she grumbled.

"How about right here and right now?" His head settled on the pillow next to hers. "I figure this is the one place I can catch you alone and conduct a conversation you can't run from."

"There's nothing stopping me from getting up and leaving."

"I'm stopping you," he immediately contradicted. His trunklike arms tightening around her. She had to admit, as unbreakable barricades went, they were fairly impressive. "You and I are staying put until we've settled our differences."

She shouldn't find the threat so appealing. But she did. "Nanna won't approve," she warned.

"Who the hell do you think gave me the idea?"

It took her a minute to digest that one. "Devious old woman."

"But smart." He lapsed into silence, simply holding her. She didn't know whether it was the warmth of his body, or the calming give-and-take of his breathing, or the slow, steady beat of his heart, but she gradually relaxed into his embrace. The minute her tension eased, he spoke again. "Okay, honey. Hit me. You're pregnant. It's my baby. The sensible choice is for us to marry."

"Sensible." She didn't care for the taste of the word.

"Yes, sensible. Now tell me why a marriage between us won't work."

"There's too much past in the way," she answered promptly. "Too many fences."

"Let's take a look at those fences." He laced his fingers with hers. "There's the Disputed Land."

"That's one."

"Our affair becoming public knowledge all those years ago."

"That's another."

"And the fact that I killed Paps."

She shifted within his hold, rolling onto her back. "I told you I didn't blame you for his death anymore."

"I appreciate that." He lifted onto one elbow and she could sense him gathering his words, searching for the right approach. "I know you adored Paps, Raine. With the exception of Nanna, you knew him better than anyone. So let me ask you this... Do you really think he'd have wanted to keep us apart after all these years? After all we've been through?"

Raine fell silent as she considered his questions. At eighteen, Paps would have moved heaven and earth to prevent a relationship between them. She'd always been grateful that he'd never found out about the night she'd spent with Lucien at the line shack. But a dozen years had passed since then. After all that time, Paps would have accepted the inevitable. Once he'd seen how she and Lucien felt, he'd have encouraged the relationship. And if he'd been standing in front of her now, knowing she carried Lucien's child, he'd have insisted on a wedding.

"Paps would have wanted us to marry," she admitted.

"You got that right. Next fence."

"People gossiped about us. I know it shouldn't matter, but—"

"I want you to listen to me, and listen good. I swear to you on everything I hold sacred, I never told anyone about our night at the line shack. Why would I? You were the woman I wanted to marry. I was intent on protecting you, not betraying you. Despite that, word got out. When I heard the talk, I admit I busted a few heads, which no doubt confirmed the story. But at twenty-one, I guess I was trying to be noble or some such nonsense."

"Apparently you haven't outgrown noble. Do I need to mention Buster's poor nose?"

He chuckled, the sound low and intimate. "Fair enough. Though at the risk of tarnishing my knightly armor, I'm happy to latch onto almost any excuse if it means I get to pound on Buster's face."

"Let's agree that's two fences down and let it go at that, shall we?" she suggested dryly. "That still leaves the Disputed Land."

"If we marry it won't be an issue any longer, will it? Kincaid land and Featherstone will become one. We'll let our children duke out ownership." At the mention of children, he cupped her belly, his hand splayed low on her abdomen. "Tell me something, Raine. How do you feel about the baby?"

There was an agonizing vulnerability in his question that cried out for complete and utter honesty. She covered his hands with her own, holding them close to where new life flourished. "I couldn't be happier. I've always wanted children."

His mouth found hers in the darkness. It was the softest of caresses, gentle and tender and loving. "I seem to recall telling you I didn't want children. At the time, I thought it was the truth."

Tears gathered in her eyes. "And now?"

"I want this baby, Raine. And I want you for the mother of my children. Can't you see? Marriage between us is the sensible option. It's the right thing to do for the baby, as well as for us."

"Sensible." He'd said that before.

Raine fought to draw breath. He wasn't offering love, but practicality. He wanted to marry her, not because he adored her or couldn't keep his hands off her or because theirs was a passion that transcended time and circumstance, but because it was sensible. The right thing to do. To her horror, the tears slipped free, forging a molten trail past her temples and into her hair.

"You don't have to answer right away," he said. "Think about it."

She fought to keep her voice from betraying her pain. "I appreciate your understanding."

"Aw, hell. I'm not handling this very well, am I?" He rolled over, bracing his elbows on either side of her shoulders and forking his fingers into her hair. "What I mean is—"

She felt his arms tense and broke into speech. "I need you to leave now."

"Your hair's wet." His concern was unmistakable. "Why is your hair wet? Are you...crying?"

"Ignore it. It's hormones."

He reared back. "Don't lie to me. It's not hormones. You never cry. You didn't even cry at your grandfather's funeral." He drew a sharp breath. "You don't want to marry me. That's why you're so upset, isn't it?"

"I—" For the first time ever, her voice let her down and she covered her face with her hands. "Please, go."

"No. I'm not leaving you like this."

She was rapidly losing control. "Please. I can't— Tomorrow," she gasped out. "We'll talk in the morning."

"You're right. We will talk in the morning. But I'm not leaving your side between now and then." He sounded oddly indignant. "What sort of man do you take me for?"

A chuckle escaped through her tears. "You're being protective again, aren't you?"

"Damn straight." He settled her into his arms and stroked her back in a soothing gesture. "Some men might run at the first sign of waterworks. But I'm not one of them. No, sirree."

"I'm scaring you, aren't I?"

"Spitless. But if you want to cry some more, go right ahead," he offered gruffly. "I'll do my best to cover any lapse in tough-guy behavior with a lot of cussing and swaggering and a manly belch or two."

Amusement won out, but she was too upset for that to last long. Her laugh turned to a sob and she buried her head against his shoulder, soaking him with her tears. He held her the entire time, being practical and sensible, not to mention noble and protective. When the final tear was spent, he wiped her cheeks with the corner of the sheet. Kissing her with a painful lack of passion, he tucked her close to his side.

"This is my fault," he informed her grimly. "Nanna warned me, but did I listen? Hell, no. I decided to do it my way. Well, come tomorrow that's going to change. I'm telling you the truth and hang the consequences."

She wanted to reply, wanted desperately to get him to

explain his comment. But she didn't have the energy. As an exhausted sleep claimed her, she couldn't help wondering....

What hadn't he told her?

CHAPTER TEN

RAINE awoke the next morning to find Lucien gone and the sun well up. She didn't waste any time, but showered and dressed with all due speed. The last comment Lucien had made before she'd fallen asleep was that he had something to tell her. She also had a vague recollection of his mentioning a mysterious warning coming from Nanna. Before another hour passed, she intended to discover the nature of that warning, as well as what deep, dark secret he'd been keeping from her.

Clattering down the steps to the main level, she nearly collided with Lucien as he entered through the front door. He caught her around the waist, his gaze sweeping her with unusual sharpness. "You okay?"

She offered a reassuring smile. "No more tears, you'll be relieved to know."

"I am relieved." His hand lingered at her waist as though he were loathe to break the contact between them. "Where are you off to in such a hurry?"

"To find you." She glanced out the open door, surprised to see Poke and Tickle saddled and ready for riding. "We going somewhere?"

"I packed breakfast in the saddlebags and thought we could head out to the north pasture and eat there for a change."

She lifted an eyebrow. "Is that where you plan to tell me whatever you've been keeping secret all this time?"

The beginning of a frown built across his brow. "I wasn't sure you heard me last night."

"Oh, I heard."

"Fair enough." He didn't sound upset, but she caught a grim quality humming beneath the surface, and it worried her. "Do you still have my work journal? You said you'd rescued it from the fire."

The secret was in his journal? Made sense, she supposed, considering he'd risked his life going after it. "I have it in my office. I've been meaning to give it to you, but I kept forgetting."

She led the way to the small study and crossed to her desk. Opening the bottom drawer, she pulled out the leather daybook. A folded piece of paper fluttered from between the pages and drifted toward the floor. Lucien grabbed for it at the same instant she did. They both missed and the paper hit the carpet, opening just enough for her to read the first few lines. Her heart rate kicked up a notch as a horrible suspicion took hold. She took a step back, leaving it where it lay. She didn't want to touch it, or look at it, or have anything to do with it, not if it meant having her hunch confirmed.

Lucien must have sensed her reaction. "Pick it up," he insisted.

She spared him a swift glance. His face was wiped clean of expression, every scrap of emotion concealed behind a stoic mask. Slowly, she bent and retrieved the paper. It didn't take long to scan the single page and confirm the contents.

It was Buck Kincaid's letter to Nanna, giving her the Disputed Land.

Raine stared at the neatly typed words for an endless minute, refusing to accept what she was reading. "You had it," she whispered hoarsely. "I don't know how you came by it, but you had it in your possession all along, didn't you?"

"Yes."

Raine fingered the official imprint of the notary seal authenticating Buck Kincaid's signature. He'd signed over the Disputed Land the day they'd buried Paps. How Lucien had gotten his hands on it after that, she couldn't imagine. But there was no denying fact.

"Tell me you just recently found this." She racked her brains for a reasonable explanation for his having Nanna's letter, desperate to give him an out. "Tell me your grandmother somehow stole it from us and that you didn't know you had it in your possession when you forced Nanna to give up her land."

"It was given to me a year ago."

She couldn't believe it, didn't want to believe it. "Then it's all been a lie. Every bit of it. Claiming there was no letter. Claiming that the land belonged to you. No wonder you felt perfectly safe demanding that Nanna return the Disputed Land. As long as you held the letter, she couldn't prove ownership."

"There's more to it than that."

She released an incredulous laugh. "More? This is plenty, thanks all the same." Anger ripped through her, desperate for release. "How could you? You stole our land. You drove posts and strung wire to fence the Featherstones off what was rightfully theirs. And you added to our financial burden by taking away our main source of water."

"Are you going to give me a chance to explain?"

"Are you going to give us back our land?" she shot back.

He shook his head. "I can't."

"Then there's nothing left to be said."

She brushed past him, intent on getting as far from Lucien as possible. Before she could make good her escape, he caught her arm. He drew her close, taking unfair advantage of his larger size and ability. She fell against his chest, bracketed by tension-ridden muscle and sinew.

How much difference a few hours made. Just last night he'd held her in these same powerful arms. But then he'd used his strength for her benefit, instead of against her. He'd seen her at her most defenseless and comforted her with breathtaking tenderness. For the first time since she'd been a teenager, she'd dropped her guard, allowing Lucien closer than any other man she'd ever known. And how had he repaid her? He'd chosen that moment of utter vulnerability to strike at the very heart of all she held dear.

"There's more to this than you understand," he repeated.

"Let go, Kincaid. I understand all I need to."

"What, no questions, Raine? No doubts? I'm guilty and that's the end of it?" Disillusionment glittered in his dark gaze. "Or are you looking for an excuse to throw up more fences? I knocked them all down last night and you need to build new ones before I have a chance to step foot on Featherstone property. Is that how it works?"

"That's right. Just consider me one giant No Trespassing sign."

A muscle jerked in his jaw. "When does it end? When do we start working in concert instead of in opposition? When do you trust me, despite all the evidence to the contrary?"

"What about you?" she demanded unevenly. "Marriage to me would solve all your problems, wouldn't it? You'd get all our land for the price of a simple 'I do.' And not just the Disputed Land, but every last rock, tree and blade of grass. Hell, Kincaid. For a deal like that,

I'm surprised you didn't call in the Cupid Committee yourself.''

"Woman, there are days when you really try my patience.''

"I'm going to try more than that.''

She tugged free of his grasp and made a beeline for the front door. Grabbing her hat on the way out, she crossed to where Tickle and Poke were patiently waiting. Snatching up the reins, she vaulted into the saddle. Lucien came right behind. Before he could climb onto Poke, Raine gave his horse a slap on its rump.

"Home, Poke-a-long," she ordered. The horse instantly obeyed. Wheeling in the opposite direction, he charged in the general direction of Kincaid land. Raine jammed her Stetson tight on her head and addressed Lucien. "You knocked down one fence too many when you told me about Nanna's letter. You should have left that one standing, Kincaid.''

"Nanna said otherwise.''

"Well for the first time in seventy-two years, Nanna is wrong. There are some secrets that should stay just that. Secret. If I hadn't known the truth I probably would have married you and filled our home with fat, happy babies.''

A fierce emotion slipped across the hard planes of his face, vanishing before she could identify it. "Thanks," he said dispassionately enough. "But I'll settle for the one already in the works.''

There was nothing she could say to that. She turned Tickle in the direction of the Disputed Land and took off, riding hard. The mare picked up on her distress and exploded in a fierce exercise of heart, muscle and speed. It wasn't until Raine considered the risk to her pregnancy that she checked up, cursing herself roundly for the foolhardiness of her actions.

Topping the ridge overlooking the river that separated Featherstone property from Kincaid, Raine switched her attention to the stretch of fence blocking her passage to the river. A painful longing filled her. Lucien couldn't know how much that land meant to her and Nanna, or he'd never have taken it. Even he couldn't be that cruel.

And yet, he had. The familiar swish of Tickle's tail helped focus her thoughts. Why had Lucien stolen their land, other than the obvious reason—greed? It didn't make sense. He wasn't a greedy man, which meant he'd have to believe that property rightfully belonged to the Kincaids. Still, that didn't explain the timing. Why make a move now, after all these years?

Drawing a deep breath, she set her sights on the Disputed Land. Whatever reason Lucien had for his actions, she wouldn't be kept off her property any longer. Urging Tickle forward, she retrieved her rope and looped one end over the nearest fence post. Dallying the slack around the saddlehorn, she utilized horse power to yank post from earth. It slid from the ground with a groan, accompanied by the death rattle of barbed wire.

What, no questions, Raine? No doubts? I'm guilty and that's the end of it?

Lucien's question rang in her head and her mouth tightened. Yes, he was guilty. And yes, that was the end of it. So what if she was being pigheaded? So what if she'd refused to hear him out? What more was there to say?

And yet part of her did have doubts. They grew softly. Quietly. Insistently. And it was that part that flinched from the memory of what she'd seen in Lucien's eyes. The pain. The disillusionment. She'd hurt him and she hated the feeling, particularly when he was so clearly in the wrong. Dammit! The pain and disillusionment should be hers to wallow in, not his. Ripping off her hat, she wiped her brow with her sleeve. There was only one problem with the stance she'd taken.

If she were in the right, then why did she feel guilty?

Retrieving her rope, she moved methodically down the line wresting post after post from the ground until they lay like a row of huge predatory teeth covered in barbed-wire braces. By the time she'd extracted the last one, anger had turned to grief and she couldn't see through the tears. Climbing off Tickle, she sank to the ground in front of the downed fence and wiped impatiently at her cheeks.

When do you trust me, despite all the evidence to the contrary?

She had to admit, that question bothered her more than anything else he'd asked, possibly because it hit so close to home. She hadn't trusted him. Not when she'd been eighteen, and not now. And yet, all he'd ever done was try and protect her. He specialized in playing the shining knight. He'd battled to salvage her reputation and paid for it by getting thrown in a jail cell. He'd saved her from a nasty fall the night of the storm and injured his wrist. He'd then rescued her from a killer tree and almost paid with his life. Every step of the way, he'd done his level best to protect her, right down to taking responsibility for their baby.

He'd even offered the protection of his name and, despite her accusation, it wasn't so he could get his hands on more Featherstone land.

It was time to face facts. Lucien was trustworthy and deep down, she knew it. That begged one important question, a question without a reasonable answer. Why?

Why had he stolen their land? She'd have sworn Lucien was too honorable to do something as criminal as that.

So, what if he hadn't?

What if she simply trusted that there was another explanation, one she should accept on faith, without his having to explain? The passing thought slipped through her head. Instead of slipping out again, it lingered, gaining strength and volume with each passing second. Finally, she couldn't ignore it any longer and forced herself to consider the possibility. If Lucien hadn't stolen the land or the letter, how did they both end up in his possession?

And then it hit her.

It didn't take Lucien long to saddle one of the Featherstone workhorses, though it felt like an eternity. Shoving his journal and the damning letter into one of the saddlebags, he mounted up. He had a fair idea where Raine had gone. Even so, he whistled for Dog as a precaution.

"Find Raine," he ordered the collie.

Dog didn't need any further prompting. He streaked from the yard, making a beeline toward the north. Lucien followed close behind. He didn't hurry. He wanted Raine to have ample opportunity to calm down before they finished their discussion. Plus, taking his time gave him a chance to think long and hard about her assertion that there were some fences that shouldn't come down. He happened to agree with her. Straightening out their differences over the Disputed Land was a necessary fence to level. But there wouldn't be any more coming down after that.

No matter what it cost, the remaining one would continue to stand untouched.

He found Raine where he'd anticipated—at the border separating Kincaid land from Featherstone. She sat huddled on the ground, posts and barbed wire heaped at her feet. She didn't look any too eager to talk and he decided a little provocation might be necessary in order to start the conversational ball rolling.

"You didn't have to rip down that fence all by yourself," he called out. "Getting rid of it was going to be one of my wedding gifts to you."

To his dismay her shoulders convulsed and she buried her head in her arms. Aw, hell. Apparently, he'd offered a bit too much provocation. Dog crept toward her, whining pitifully, while Lucien practically fell off his horse in his haste to reach her. Crouching at her side, he wrapped her up in a tight embrace. She didn't resist as he feared. With an inarticulate cry, she burrowed against him, and just like the night before, he held her until her tears were spent.

"Don't misunderstand, or think I'm ungrateful," he murmured against the top of her head. "But why are you letting me touch you? I figured at the very least you were going to add another lump to my nose."

"I've been thinking."

"And that's a good thing, right?"

"Should have been. Would have been real good, if I hadn't realized what a sorry excuse for a human being I am." She stirred in his arms. "I owe you an apology, Lucien. I should have trusted you. I won't make that mistake again."

Relief swept over him. It was going to work out. Somehow, some way, they'd reach an understanding. He just needed to take it one careful step at a time. "Don't, honey," he murmured against her temple. "It's not worth it. It's just a piece of land. It was there long before us and it'll still be there long after we're gone.''

"You're wrong, Lucien. That piece is special.''

"Why? Can you explain it to me?''

Her throat worked. "We scattered Paps' ashes along that stretch.''

Lucien flinched. "I'm so sorry, Raine. I had no idea. She never said or I wouldn't—'' He swallowed the rest of his words, calling himself every manner of fool.

With a quick sweep of her hand, she dislodged his hat. "Nanna never told you about Paps, or you wouldn't have bought the land from her? That's the piece of this puzzle I'm missing, isn't it?'' Sunlight cut across his face, brutal and unrelenting, allowing her to read a truth he couldn't bring himself to speak. "Nanna's the one who gave you the letter. She approached you a year ago when our financial situation reached the critical point, didn't she? And you bought the Disputed Land from her.''

He rubbed a hand along the nape of his neck. "Yeah. Something like that.''

"I gather she asked you not to tell me the truth?''

"She requested I keep it quiet and I agreed. I suspect she was hoping you'd come after me when you heard about the change of ownership and demand an explanation. Maybe it was her way of throwing the two of us together. You and I would be forced into a long overdue confrontation.'' He regarded her curiously. "What clued you in?''

She swept off her own hat and tossed it on top of his. The sunlight slanted across her features with the same brutality it had his, accentuating the emotions she struggled so hard to control. She looked exhausted. "I started wondering why you'd keep such a damning piece of evidence, particularly if you'd come by it illicitly. Only a complete idiot would have held on to the thing instead of tossing it on the nearest bonfire.''

"Gee, thanks.''

A smile eclipsed her tears. ''Since you're not a complete idiot, there had to be another explanation.'' Her smile faded. ''And then there was the house fire. Something kept bothering me about that. Why, of all the valuables you could have chosen to rescue, would you go after the letter?''

Heaven help their children if they ever tried to keep a secret from Raine. She'd figure out the truth before they so much as opened their mouths. ''And what did you conclude?''

"Once I realized Nanna had sold the land to you, I could only come up with one reason you'd hang on to the letter.''

"Sentimental attachment?'' he offered diffidently.

"Hardly. I'm guessing—'' Her voice broke and she visibly fought for control.

"Don't, sweetheart. Please, don't.'' He slid his hands along her jawline, sweeping a thumb just beneath her bottom lip in an effort to still its tremble. ''It's not worth all this heartache.''

If anything, the tremble worsened. ''Yes, it is. It's past time we finish this.''

He closed his eyes, but it didn't help. He was too sharply attuned to her pain to shut it out. He could still see the sorrow lining the striking planes of her face, hear the ache etched into her words, feel the tension ridging the muscles along her neck and arms. He took it all in and made it his own. ''Then get it done so we can move on.''

"I'm guessing that at some point—probably after

Nanna was gone and could no longer object—you planned for that letter to mysteriously resurface. Then you'd return the land, no one the wiser.'' She searched his face through her tears. ''Am I right?''

''I might have been playing with an idea similar to that. But it's over now. Once we're married it won't be an issue any longer.''

''It'll never be over. Not as long as we continue to have fences between us.''

He forced a smile. ''Not a problem. You've taken care of them. No more fences.''

''No?''

Her skepticism ate at him and he slowly released her, tempted to blurt out the rest, even the part he'd sworn he wouldn't. ''Raine—'' She cut him off before he could attempt something so ill-advised.

''You accused me of not trusting you, and you were right.'' Her shoulders moved in an agitated shrug. ''I don't know anymore, Lucien. Maybe we've lived on opposite sides of a fence too long to trust each other.''

He didn't pretend to misunderstand. ''I've always accused you of putting up fences, like it was a bad thing.'' He chose his words with care. ''But sometimes they're needed. They protect people from hurt.''

''And you're big on protecting people, aren't you?''

''Sometimes.'' Dog approached, worrying at his hand, and he scratched the animal's ruff. ''When I care about them.''

''Which is why you didn't tell me the truth about the Disputed Land.''

''Yes.''

She studied him in silence for a moment. Her eyes were filled with sunshine, turning the color to a translucent shade of green. He could see her every thought and emotion reflected there. Even as he watched comprehension dawned. "There's something more. Something you're not telling me. What else are you protecting me from?"

Dog whined, pawing at Lucien's shirt. Gently he set Raine aside and stood, shooing off the collie. "I suggest we put this nonsense behind us and talk about where we go from here."

"Nonsense?" she repeated. Her eyes narrowed over his choice of words, but she answered mildly enough. "I guess that depends on whether we're planning to live our lives on opposite sides of a fence."

"You said yourself, some fences shouldn't come down." The words had scarcely left his mouth before Dog was all over him, barking in agitation. Leaping at him, the collie snagged his shirt and pulled it loose. Lucien took a quick step back, staring at the animal in disbelief. "What's wrong with you, you crazy mutt? I thought we were buddies."

"He's not happy with you for some reason." Raine studied him with rapt attention. "Maybe because I'm not."

He checked his shirt for damage. "Well, call him off before he rips something."

"Maybe if you answer my question he'll leave you alone. 'Fess up, Kincaid. What else are you keeping from me?"

How did she do it? He'd sworn he wouldn't allow her anywhere near his last fence. He wasn't even willing to admit there was a last fence. Yet, there she stood, rope in hand, ready to drop her lasso over post and wire and yank them from the ground.

"It has nothing to do with us. And nothing to do with our baby. Instead of dwelling on what's over and done

with, we should be looking to the future. Our future."
Giving the collie a wide berth, he approached Raine,
tugging her to her feet. "Now I'm asking you straight-
out. Will you marry me?"

"Because of the baby? Because—" She cocked her
head to one side. "Now, how did you phrase it last
night? Because it's the sensible thing to do?"

"Aw, hell. Is that how it came across?" He exhaled
roughly. "Sweetheart, I've wanted you for my wife
since you were eighteen and I was a lovesick twenty-
one-year-old. I haven't stopped loving you in all the
years since. Can't you tell just looking at me? I'm a
useless wreck of a man, I'm so crazy in love with you.
I've loved you all my life, and I'll keep loving you until
the day my ashes are scattered alongside Paps'."

She burned with an inner radiance. "Love, not ex-
pediency?"

He gathered her hands in his. "Love first, last and
foremost. Marry me, Raine. Not because it's sensible.
Not because of the baby. Marry me because you love
me and want to fill our home with all those fat, happy
babies you mentioned earlier. One or a dozen, doesn't
make no nevermind to me, so long as you're their
mother, as well as my wife."

He could see her agreement gleaming in her eyes,
could practically hear the "yes" hovering on her lips.
Before she could utter a single word, Dog snarled and
leapt at his side again, clawing feverishly. This time, he
snagged Lucien's shirt, tearing a long rent along one
seam.

Raine's agreement died unspoken. "What's going on,
Lucien?" she demanded.

He backed away, clamping a hand to his side. "I don't
know what you're talking about."

She came charging after him, step for step. Before he could stop her, she grabbed his shirt and ripped apart the snaps. Skinning the heavy cotton half off him, she scanned first his arms, then his chest. Finally, her gaze lit on the scar marring his side. He sucked in air and waited, waited for the future he'd fought so hard to create to come to a truly bad end.

Raine reached out to touch the old wound, hesitating at the last instant. Her breath escaped in an unsteady rush. "You never told me how you came by that scar."

His hands collapsed into fists. "Let it drop, woman."

"You said you were gored. But this is no goring."

"I told you. A man doesn't like talking about his moments of incompetence."

"You're so full of it, Kincaid. This isn't from a bull or any other critter roaming your ranch. You think I haven't seen the aftermath of a shotgun blast before?" She glared at him, her eyes blazing with emotion. "What happened? Who did this?"

He swept his shirt closed. "It was an accident."

It was absolutely, without question, the wrong word to use. Shock held her frozen in place. "An accident? Like the accident with Paps?"

"Raine—"

"You got this the day he died, didn't you?" When Lucien didn't answer, she snatched his shirt open again and frantically examined the scar. "Did he get a round off after you shot him?"

"No."

"But he did this." She wrapped her hands around Lucien's shirt and shook him. "He shot you, didn't he? Don't lie to me, Lucien. I can tell from your expression that I'm right."

He focused on a spot over her left shoulder. "Let it go."

"But...why? Why would Paps shoot you in an argument over the Disputed Land? Buck, I could understand. But why you?" When he didn't answer, she grabbed his face and forced him to look at her. "The argument was over the Disputed Land, wasn't it? Your fight with Paps?"

Lucien simply shook his head.

"Then—" Her eyes widened and she fell back, stumbling in her haste. "No. Oh, no."

"Don't." She was killing him, inch by inch. "No more, do you hear me?"

But she was too distraught to listen. "He went over there because he found out about the night we spent at the line shack, didn't he? He was going after you because we'd slept together. What happened was all my fault. He died because of me."

"Stop it!" The truth burned for release, welling up inside and erupting after years of pent-up pain and pressure. "Your grandfather died because he was a fool. He didn't need to use a gun to force me to marry you. I'd have done anything—anything—to make you my wife. He was wild that day, ranting and raving, and insisting we get married before the sun set. I'd just been released from jail after my run-in with Buster and wasn't thinking too straight. I vaguely recall saying something that ticked him off and he shook his gun at me. Hell, honey. That shotgun was so old I'm surprised it still remembered how to fire. It went off and the edge of the blast scraped my side."

"That's no scrape!"

"Nor was it life-threatening. Paps never meant to shoot me. It was an accident. But afterward..." Lucien closed his eyes and ran a weary hand across his brow. "I'll regret to the day I die what went down after that. I should have backed off. Played dead. Anything. Instead, I rushed him and tried to wrestle his gun away. After that... Well, you know the rest."

"Why didn't you tell us what really happened? Why have you kept silent all this time?"

"Paps was a good man. The best. I couldn't tarnish his name and reputation over one mistake. I couldn't—" He broke off and bowed his head, the air shuddering from his lungs.

"You couldn't knock the man I adored off his pedestal," she finished for him. "So you took the blame."

"I was going to tell you." He crossed to his horse and opened one of the saddlebags. Pulling out his work journal he gave it to Raine. "It's in there. All of it."

She carefully opened the volume. The initial entries were all work related, each dated shortly before the day Paps had died. She thumbed through them until she reached a section that contained a rambling note, written in Lucien's distinctive handwriting. It was a love letter, fierce and passionate and devoted. And it detailed every bit of the events from that long-ago day.

Words leapt out at her. Words like responsibility and regret and love. Words filled with an agonizing despair. "You never sent this note." It hurt to speak.

"I couldn't."

More letters followed, revisions of the first, filled with scratch marks and long, poignant passages that he'd later crossed out. She continued to read, slowly turning page after page. With each new note, the tenor gradually altered. Instead of desperately trying to explain what had happened, he took the blame. References to his having been shot vanished, as did the reason for the fight. The very last letter completed the process—the knight had emerged, intent on protecting those he loved.

The final note was the one he'd sent to her and Nanna.

After she'd finished reading the last word Raine walked into his arms and clung to him. "Is this the last of it?" she demanded brokenly. "Are all the secrets in the open now?"

"There aren't any more. I swear."

Anger competed with her tears. "I love you, Kincaid. But if you ever try and play the part of the protective knight again, you won't walk straight for a month. You got that?"

"From now on, you can rescue me." He took her mouth in a lingering kiss before sweeping her into his arms and lowering her to the ground. He followed her down, resting his head against her belly. "You never answered my question, Raine. Will you marry me?"

Slipping her hands through his hair, she held him tight against his child, and smiled through her tears. "Of course, I'll marry you."

He lifted his head and looked at her. "And are you agreeing because of the baby? Or because it's sensible?"

"To be honest, marrying you is probably the least sensible thing I'll ever do." Her smile grew. "But when you're crazy in love, who cares about being sensible?"

He shifted upward and kissed her before the last word had died. Kissed her gently in a final farewell to the past. Kissed her in gratitude for her generosity and understanding. Kissed her passionately, as a man does the woman he loves more than life itself. He kissed her with all the pent-up need of a man who'd walked in darkness for too many years and come within inches of losing his heart and soul.

"No more fences," she whispered.

"You pulled down the last one. I promise."

For endless moments, they simply held each other, two wayward lovers who'd found their other half. Where opposition had locked them in dispute, now love would seal them in an unbreakable bond.

Finally Lucien lifted onto one elbow. "You know, we still haven't discussed names for the baby." He hesitated a moment before casually offering, "If we have a girl, how about we name her after Nanna?"

She understood why he was making the offer and a fierce joy filled her. But his suggestion also made her chuckle. "It's a sweet thought, but are you sure you want to name our daughter Sunflower?"

He blanched before making a gallant recovery. "Sunflower. Er, great name. We could call her Sunny for short. Sunny Kincaid. Memorable, don't you think? And if it's a boy, we'll name him in honor of Paps. What do you say?"

"I'm not sure that's such a good idea," she demurred.

"Why not? His name can't be worse than Sunflower."

"I guess that depends on your perspective."

"I'm trying to do the noble thing here. Throw me a bone, will you?" He shoved an eager Dog aside. "No, not you. This bone's for me. After what you pulled, you can go find your own."

She shrugged. "Okay. Since you insist, we'll name our son after Paps. But don't say I didn't warn you."

He loomed above her, planting his hands on either side of her head. "Come on, honey. Spit it out. What will I be calling the boy? Poindexter? Yogi? Archibald?" His brows drew together. "Please tell me it's not some girly name like Mary or Leslie. Anything's better than that."

"I'm relieved to hear you say that, because it's definitely not a girly name."

"Raine!"

She choked on a laugh. "Okay, but don't forget this was your idea." A delicious combination of love and laughter glittered in her eyes. "If we have a boy, you'll be calling him Buster."

EPILOGUE

SHADOE poured champagne into a pair of crystal flutes and carried them to where Adelaide stood beneath an arbor of roses. Their rich scent filled the air, underscoring the perfume from the dozens of flower arrangements that filled the garden setting. "I have to hand it to you, boss lady. I didn't think we'd pull this one off."

His mother accepted one of the gently fizzing glasses and smiled benevolently in the direction of Raine and Lucien. They'd paused for pictures within the embrace of a flower-bedecked arch similar to the one screening her. Above their heads was an upturned silver horseshoe—her wedding present to them. On one side were Tess and her husband, Shadyde, while Emma and Gray stood on the other.

"We almost didn't pull it off," she replied. "I must say, the timing of those letters proved fortuitous."

"You were the one who told me when to send them." He shot her a speculative look. "Did you know there was a storm moving in?"

She dismissed the question out of hand. "How would I know that? I was nowhere in the vicinity."

"If you say so." He watched as Lucien bent to kiss his bride, one hand around her waist, the other settled protectively over the slight bulge at her middle. "I wonder what would have happened if they hadn't been trapped by that storm."

"Fortunately, we don't have to worry about that."

"True." He drained his glass and gave his mother a curious look. "So who's next on our list?"

Adelaide lifted an eyebrow. "Are you that anxious to get back to work?"

An attractive blonde chose that moment to stroll by. She offered Shadoe a warm, come-hither smile and he handed his empty champagne flute to his mother. "I guess work can wait. In the meantime, I see a yellow rose of Texas that needs plucking." He gave her a quick peck on the cheek. "Excuse me, won't you?"

The moment he disappeared into the crowd, a figure stepped from the shadows, a cigar clamped between his teeth and a walking stick swinging from one hand. "We did good, didn't we, Addie?" he asked as he joined her. "Your boy didn't suspect a thing."

She smiled. "I seem to recall telling you to watch from the sidelines and not get directly involved. You don't listen very well, do you?"

"I have no idea what you're talking about," he retorted. If it hadn't been for the hint of bluster in his voice, she might have believed him.

"I'm talking about the timing of that note and the way those horses bolted. It had a familiar feel to it." She lifted an eyebrow. "Your fine hand, I presume?"

He gathered his walking stick in two hands and executed a perfect golf stroke, smoothly decapitating one of the roses decorating the trellis overhead. The blossom fluttered earthward and he caught it before it could hit the ground. "Let's just that when I set my mind to something, I see to it that it gets done." He offered the flower to Adelaide. "No half measures for Thomas T. Palmer."

Her smile grew. "You, Tee, are a flirt."

"No question there, my dear." He studied the glowing tip of his cigar. "I have to tell you, Addie, I'm tired of retirement. It doesn't agree with me. So what do you say? Are you satisfied? You willing to make me one of your personal cupids?''

''Without question. In fact, I need someone special for our next couple of assignments.'' She slipped her hand into the crook of his arm. ''I understand you're about to become a great-grandfather. Is it true?''

Tee's chest swelled. ''So Emma claims. She was under orders to deliver a great-grandbaby nine months to the day after her wedding, and by golly, I believe she intends to do it.''

Adelaide glanced across the lawn to where Shadoe stood. The blonde had disappeared, replaced by a stunning redhead. ''Well, I'm not quite ready to become a great-grandmother, but I do have a hankering to become a grandmother. And since none of my children appear inclined to grant my wish, I'll have to see if I can't instigate it on my own.''

Tee followed her gaze and his face creased in a broad grin. ''Your son? He's our next assignment?''

''Oh, not just my son. I also have a daughter. And she's an even bigger challenge than he is.'' She leaned closer. ''Are you up for it?''

''That depends. Do I get to fight dirty?''

Adelaide chuckled. ''Is there any other way?''

''Well then, I know the perfect place to buy all those baby doodads and geegaws you'll be needing. Because if I were a betting man—'' he grinned around his cigar ''—which I am, I'd lay odds that you'll be a grandma before another year goes by.''

Raine double checked to make sure all was quiet in the nursery before returning to the e-mail she'd been writing to Tess and Emma.

Now, where was I? Oh, right. So, we named our daughter Sunny, which is short for Sunflower in honor of Nanna. If I have a boy someday, we'll name him after Paps. Whenever my darling husband gets a little bossy or overprotective, I just call our daughter, "Buster." Poor Lucien goes green around the gills. It's an interesting sight. Maybe that's because Buster is the name of this really annoying individual who likes to make rude remarks and has a tendency to break noses—usually Lucien's. Or maybe it's because I told him that Buster was my grandfather's name. (One of these days I'll have to tell him it's really John. But not quite yet.)

Emma, thank you for sending the video of little Tommy T. It was so cool seeing him take his first steps. Not even a year old and he's already walking like a pro. Honestly, if I didn't know better I'd swear he'd been doing it for weeks. Maybe months.

And, Tess, have you started picking out baby names? I know, I know. You haven't told us you're pregnant, yet. But Nanna said you were and… well…you know Nanna. If she says you're pregnant, you might as well start shopping for cribs. Oh, and she says, think blue. (Hint, hint.)

Okay, got to run. Hey! I have an idea. If our kids aren't married by the time they reach thirty, why don't we make a pact to call in the Cupid Committee?

                                        Love, Raine

P.S. I was just kidding about the Cupid Committee.
P.P.S. Sort of!

A brand-new title by

Betty Neels

With more than 134 novels to her name,
international bestselling author **Betty Neels**
has left a legacy of wonderful romances
to enjoy, cherish and keep.

Curl up this winter and enjoy
the enchantment of a Christmas
never to be forgotten, with
the magic of a mistletoe marriage...

THE FORTUNES OF FRANCESCA

Professor Marc van der Kettener has been
a helping hand since he met Francesca—but
now he's proposed! Francesca is torn: is Marc
simply helping her out of a tight spot again,
or has he really fallen in love?

On sale December 2002 (#3730)

Don't miss this tantalizing Christmas treat from

HARLEQUIN®
Romance®

EMOTIONALLY EXHILARATING!

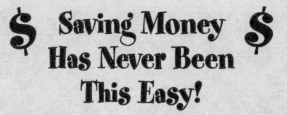

$ Saving Money $
Has Never Been
This Easy!

Just fill out and send in this form from any
October, November and December 2002 books
and we will send you a coupon booklet worth a
total savings of $20.00 off future purchases of
Harlequin and Silhouette books in 2003.

Yes! It's that easy!

I accept your incredible offer!
Please send me a coupon booklet:

Name (PLEASE PRINT)

Address   Apt. #

City   State/Prov.   Zip/Postal Code

In a typical month, how many
Harlequin and Silhouette novels do you read?
❑ 0-2   ❑ 3+

097KJKDNC7   097KJKDNDP

Please send this form to:
   In the U.S.: Harlequin Books, P.O. Box 9071, Buffalo, NY 14269-9071
   In Canada: Harlequin Books, P.O. Box 609, Fort Erie, Ontario L2A 5X3

Allow 4-6 weeks for delivery. Limit one coupon booklet per household. Must be
postmarked no later than January 15, 2003.

HARLEQUIN®
Makes any time special®

Silhouette®
Where love comes alive™

© 2002 Harlequin Enterprises Limited   PHQ402